GHOST Voyages

CORA TAYLOR

Cover by
Marc Sorozan

Scholastic Canada Ltd.

Scholastic Canada Ltd.
123 Newkirk Road, Richmond Hill, Ontario, Canada L4C 3G5

Scholastic Inc.
730 Broadway, New York, NY 10003, USA

Ashton Scholastic Pty Limited
PO Box 579, Gosford, NSW 2250, Australia

Ashton Scholastic Limited
Private Bag 1, Penrose, Auckland, New Zealand

Scholastic Publications Ltd.
Villiers House, Clarendon Avenue, Leamington Spa, Warwickshire,
CV32 5PR, UK

This book is based on the short story "Jeremy Finds the Door," which appeared in *Canadian Living*, July 1990.

The author wishes to acknowledge the assistance of the St. Albert Public Library Writer-in-Residence Programme.

Quote on pages 90-91 from *The Charlton 1982 Canada Stamp and Storybook* by James Montagnes, courtesy The Charlton Press.
Stamps reproduced courtesy Canada Post Corporation.

Canadian Cataloguing in Publication Data

Taylor, Cora, 1936-
Ghost voyages

ISBN 0-590-74058-X

I. Title.

PS8589.A85G5 1992 jC813'.52 C91-095741-X
PZ7.C35Lu 1990

6 5 4 3 2 1 Printed in Canada 2 3 4 5 6/9
Manufactured by Gagné Printing

To my grandsons
Jeremy René Thomas
and
Charles Wellington Thomas

1.

It all started with the boxes that were shipped to Edmonton from Great-Granny Stark's house. The usual sort of things that an old person accumulates. Junk, as far as Jeremy could see. Personal belongings, his mother said. The sort of thing the old lady couldn't take into the nursing home.

He hadn't been very interested. Not even when his mother got all excited over the box with the stamp albums.

"Look at this! It's the old stamp album I had when I was your age," she said.

Jeremy couldn't see much to get excited about. The album wasn't very big. There were pictures of stamps to show you what to fill in, but they were still waiting for the right stamp. When he turned the pages it seemed to him that hardly any of the spaces had been used, except in the Canadian section. It must have been discouraging, he thought, if you had stamps that didn't fit. On one page his mother had glued in a blank sheet filled with left-over stamps.

"Doesn't look like a very good book, if you had no place to put all those stamps," he said.

His mother shrugged, "I know. I almost gave it up and then I got the idea that I'd *specialize* . . . you know, just collect a certain kind of stamp. I did flowers and birds, I remember. . . . " She flipped open the second book, which wasn't a proper stamp album like the other but a big blue scribbler with a hard cover. On the front in careful block letters Jeremy could see the words: "MY OWN PERSONAL FAVOURITE STAMPS — Property of Sandra Stark — DO NOT TOUCH!"

Inside there were pages and pages of beautiful stamps. Exotic birds and flowers from countries Jeremy had never heard of, along with a few Canadian flowers. There was a pretty 17-cent stamp of a flower garden, but the Canadian birds — Canada jays and sparrows — looked boring beside the colourful foreign bird stamps.

Jeremy rummaged through the box. There must be something more interesting than stamps. But it seemed to be just a lot of old scribblers and school books of his mother's. Then he felt the book, almost as if it slipped into his hand somehow. It was a hardcover scribbler too, black and battered. He picked it up. The edges were soft and strangely comfortable to hold. He had the funny feeling that this book had been waiting for him.

Inside was written: "SHIPS AND BOATS AND THINGS THAT FLOAT — STAMPS — Property of Harvey Stark." And squeezed in with it: "and Sandra."

"Look Mum," he said, "this must have belonged to Grandad when he was a kid."

"Oh, my goodness!" she said softly, reaching for the book, "I wondered what happened to that!"

Jeremy didn't want to let go, the book was so . . . so . . . he couldn't explain it . . . friendly, or something.

"I remember when he gave it to me." She had a sad, remembering look in her eyes. "As if he was giving me something truly wonderful . . . " She shook her head. "But I never got very excited about his ship stamp collection. I added to it . . . ," she turned the pages slowly, " . . . here's one I put in — the *Nonsuch*." She was pointing to a five-cent stamp of an old ship, with wind-filled sails.

"That's a neat stamp all right," Jeremy said. He

liked the clear, bright colours and the ship itself, the determined way it rode the waves.

His mother nodded. "Yes, it really is. But I much preferred my birds and flowers. Still, I guess this is what gave me the idea of specializing." She shook her head sadly. "I think he was disappointed though. He used to keep asking me about them. Just about the ship stamps — he didn't seem very interested in the rest of the collection." There was a catch in her voice, almost a sob.

Oh no, Jeremy thought, now she's going to start crying. He'd been only five years old when Grandad died but he missed him too. Not like Mum of course — she still cried sometimes when something reminded her of him. She'd start out to tell him happy stories and they would laugh, and then she'd get sad because he was missing having his grandad. This time she really is going to cry, Jeremy thought, wishing she wouldn't or at least that he could think of something useful to do or say when she did.

He tried but he couldn't think of anything, so he just had to sit there while she mumbled a muffled, "Excuse me," and ran out of the room.

It was then that he found the stamp and the note. He was turning the pages of the ships and boats book, feeling better than he had all day. He'd been sentenced to a no-Nintendo weekend for promising to clean up his room and not doing it. How was a guy supposed to know when a mother said, "I'm not telling you again!" that this time she really meant it? Usually she got busy and forgot to check up on him.

He noticed something, a small envelope, the kind for a gift tag. It had writing on it, kind of shaky but easy to read. He recognized it as Granny Stark's. She must have written it and tucked it into the book and then forgotten about it.

"Do you remember the story I told you about this boat?" he read. "A little family history you may want to pass on some day." He supposed it was a note to his mother, but it didn't have her name on it so he opened the envelope. Inside there was a single stamp. A boat stamp.

And that was how it all began.

2.

It happened so suddenly, Jeremy had no time to think. One minute he was sitting quietly in his bedroom looking at the stamp. The next he was here in the dazzling sunshine hearing men's voices from somewhere below. He wasn't even sure where "here" was. A ship or boat of some sort. On a river, because he could see trees and banks on both sides.

He remembered the stamp he'd been looking at. The tiny print on the bottom said "NORTHCOTE". A river boat, an olden days river boat. There'd been something . . . he'd seen a movement . . . as if the smoke from the smokestack really was moving. And then he'd dug a magnifying glass out of another of the old boxes — and here he was! He realized that he was on an upper deck. It was a commanding view.

"I'm the King of the Castle," he thought.

He felt strange and light-headed, as if he could do anything. Then he heard somebody coming and backed away guiltily. . . .

And was back sitting at the desk in his room.

Jeremy shook his head. Weird, he thought. Am I suffering from Nintendo withdrawal or what? For two seconds I thought I was on a boat. He was sitting there stunned and puzzled when his mother came back in blowing her nose.

"Sorry about that, Jer-bear." She gave his shoulder a squeeze, picking up a large brown envelope tucked in the back of the book. The bright Canadian stamps spilled out onto the desk. "Oh, look! Granny saved all these boat stamps for me."

Jeremy was not going to look. He hated it when his mother called him Jer-Bear, as if he were three years old or something.

He was really confused by what had happened. Not that he was about to tell his mother. She'd think he was having hallucinations or sick or something and get worried.

She was picking up the stamps one by one. "I wonder how many times the *Bluenose* has been on a stamp?" she mused. "I know there was an old one somewhere and here it is again on this 37-cent stamp Granny saved." Her voice was soft. "Some of these are quite recent. She must have been cutting them off for me all along. Oh, Jer-Bear," she chuckled, "isn't it funny how grandparents think a person never grows up?"

What about parents! Jeremy thought. Was she ever going to stop the Jer-Bear bit? He'd better distract her or she'd be Jer-Bearing all night.

"That's a beautiful one," he said pointing to one of the tumbled stamps.

His mother picked it up, squinted at the tiny print and read, "Tall ships visit . . . oh, I remember seeing that on TV and wishing I could get to see those wonderful sailing ships. I guess maybe Dad was right — your grandad, I mean — thinking the ship stamps were more interesting than birds and flowers. After all, they sort of represent adventure, don't they? Most of them have stories. . . ."

"Yeah." He didn't let go of the *Northcote* stamp, but he handed her the note. "So tell me this story."

He watched as his mother picked it up and read: " . . . story I told you about this boat . . . family history . . . pass on some day." She looked at the stamp in his hand. "Isn't it awful? I remember her saying something about it, but I don't remember *exactly*. . . . I wasn't paying attention and I always thought I could ask her any time I wanted to know." She shook her head ruefully. "She was always talking about stuff I wasn't interested in at the time."

"Can't you remember *anything* about it?" Jeremy said, a little annoyed. He had hardly ever seen Great-Granny Stark but some of the family stories his mother had retold had been kind of interesting.

His mother shook her head sadly. "You know how when you're a kid you don't always listen . . ." she smiled at him, "like when I keep telling you to hang up your coat?"

He just shook his head. Sometimes he wondered if his mother had ever been a kid. Anybody knew that stories and orders were two different things. Stories you listened to.

"Let me see that stamp." It felt strange letting go of it. He almost couldn't. "Oh yes, the *Northcote*. Well, I do remember it was used in the Riel Rebellion. There were riverboats on the North and South Saskatchewan rivers in those days. I remember Granny saying that her mother talked about seeing them when *she* was a little girl. They hadn't been that convenient, the rivers were too full of sand bars and shallow spots." His mother pointed to the funny-looking "grasshopper legs" sticking out along the sides in front of the boat. "Somehow or other," she said, "they used those to lift or drag the boat over the sandbars when they got stuck. I think they even called it 'grasshoppering.' "

He waited impatiently. He couldn't wait to hold the stamp again and almost snatched it away from his mother. "That doesn't sound much like a 'story' or 'family history' to me," he grumbled.

"You're right," she said thoughtfully. "I'll try to remember while I'm getting supper."

This time he picked up the magnifying glass to look at those "grasshopper legs." Holding the stamp very carefully, he raised it to his eye. Yes, there it was again, some movement. He looked away quickly. It was the same. He held his breath, wondering if it would happen again, and looked right at the smokestack with its smoke billowing out. It was moving, puffing away, and there was the little door on the deck just below the pilot house he'd been looking at before.

3.

This time he was more prepared. But not much. Suddenly he was coming through the door onto the deck in the bright sunshine.

It must be springtime, he thought. There was that special, fresh, spring smell in the air — a kind of moist earth, growing things smell. He took a few deep breaths. He felt great, as if he could do anything. It made him feel quite daring.

At least he knew where he was this time. And sort of how he'd got here.

Except the *Northcote* did not look exactly the way it did on the stamp. Oh, the grasshopper legs were there all right, but the decks were piled high with sandbags and there were soldiers in red coats everywhere.

Jeremy was about to duck around behind one of the big smokestacks when he realized that he had nothing to hide. No body! He held his hand out in front of his face. No hand!

No wonder he felt so light and free. He must be in some kind of time warp or something. He was here on the upper deck of the *Northcote*, but his body must be back in his bedroom holding the stamp.

I'm like a ghost here, he thought. Except that a ghost is somebody coming from the past into the present and I'm doing just the opposite.

So these men must be the soldiers from the Riel Rebellion time. He wished that his mother had told him more than just the "grasshopper legs" part of the story.

He'd wondered how "grasshoppering" worked. He'd soon find out, he realized, for the boat seemed to be stuck fast on a sandbar. A line of red-coated men was unloading cargo, passing the bales and boxes hand to hand and putting them onto a barge that was still afloat beside the *Northcote*.

Jeremy guessed the other men, who weren't in uniform, must be the crew of the boat by the way they seemed to know where everything was. They were placing the long poles perpendicularly, one on either side of the boat near the front. Pulleys from the top were then wound up. He could see that, little by little, the front of the boat was being raised.

"Start the engines!" someone called.

"Give 'er steam," called another voice and the engine roared to life, the boat lurched forward, and the men moved the poles again.

Jeremy watched as this procedure was repeated. He felt sorry for the men, who were sweating in the warm, spring sunshine. It was obviously hard, boring work. Each time they did it they gained only a few metres, it seemed, and it took them four tries before they hit deep water and the *Northcote* was once more afloat.

The crewman nearest him mopped his forehead and mumbled to the man beside him, "I'll be glad when this is over. General Middleton must be mad to think he can turn a cargo boat into a warship."

His friend laughed, "Look on the bright side." He pointed to the soldiers who were now reversing the process and moving the cargo back on board the *Northcote*. "We've at least got the militia to lend a hand. . . . You and I would have *that* to do before we were through!"

"Still, I'll be happier when we can get back to our usual hauling. Our top speed is only five miles per hour at best. . . .We spend most of our time 'sparring' off sandbars. What did we do yesterday, anyway?"

"About fifteen miles."

"And look at the 'preparations.' Tore down Dumont's barn and took the planking to surround the lower deck. But the cabin walls are too thin for protection. And the pilot house . . . " He shook his head hopelessly.

"Wouldn't want to be Captain Seger and Smith up there . . . nothing but a few bags of grain and some boxes around the lower part, wide open on top," said the other man.

"Yeah, they'll be sitting ducks when the shooting starts."

Jeremy watched as things were reloaded and safely stowed. He noticed that they hadn't unloaded the heavy cannon or the funny-looking machine gun. Most of all he was just enjoying the freedom he felt in his ghostly body. It was great being invisible. He could move around right in the middle of things and no one could see him. All he had to worry about was someone bumping into him. And being invisible made him lighter. He seemed to be walking effortlessly, almost floating. It was a nice airy feeling. But something was bothering him. He wasn't sure what it was. Something to do with home.

He wished his mother had been able to tell him the story. It would be nice to know what his connection to this boat was and *then* come back and meet the person. Especially now that he knew he could come again.

The more he thought about home, the more the "something" that was bothering him did. It felt sort of like it did when he'd got into trouble in school on Friday afternoon and knew that when he got back on Monday there'd be problems. All weekend, even when he forgot about it, it was there at the back of his mind, like a worry-wart.

He knew about worry-warts. His Aunt Wendy used to call him that when he kept bugging her to take him someplace. She said a worry-wart was like when you had a sore or something in your mouth and it only hurt if you rubbed the spot, but your tongue kept reminding you because it kept touching it.

Maybe his mother had remembered something by now. And there didn't seem to be much going on. The *Northcote* was chugging slowly and steadily down the river. He might as well go home. Besides, he didn't know what would happen if his mother walked into the room when he was out of his body. Funny to think of your body like a suit of clothes. Yes, he decided, he'd go back.

And then he realized what the worry-wart was. He knew how to get here all right. Hold the stamp, see the smoke move, and look closely and — presto! here he was. What he didn't know — no wonder he'd been worried — was how to get back!

4.

For a moment he almost panicked. He'd got back once but how had he done it? It had happened too fast for him to notice. That time he'd been here and back home almost instantly.

What had he done? He'd got onto the *Northcote* each time looking at the stamp and then had ended up coming through the door on the top deck. So the first thing to do, he thought, trying hard to remain calm, was to find that door again.

He went quickly up to the deck he'd been on when he first arrived. There were two doors on the upper deck but he was sure this was the right one. If it wasn't, he'd try the other and if that didn't work . . . well, he didn't like to think about that. Being a ghost was okay but he wouldn't want it as a full-time job.

The first time he went through the door nothing happened. Perhaps he had to be going the other way. That didn't work either. Maybe just being *in* the doorway. Just move into the doorway and stand there.

It worked! He was back at his desk, holding the stamp and the magnifying glass. He set the stamp down quickly in case he took off again. For a minute he just sat there, limp with relief. It felt strange having a body once more. Lumpy.

"Jeremy!" His mother called from the foot of the stairs. "Have you got that room cleaned up yet?"

"I'm working on it!" He slowly stood up. His legs and body seemed to weigh a ton. He almost laughed, it felt so weird.

As if he were dragging weights on his feet.

"Well you've got half an hour until supper and then I'm coming up to check." She sounded annoyed.

Jeremy started shoving things into the closet. He'd take another trip on the *Northcote* after supper.

He ran downstairs just before the half hour was up. If his mother didn't have to come upstairs maybe she'd forget to check his room. It looked a *lot* better, but if she looked under the bed there'd be trouble.

"Oh good! Spaghetti. Can I have seconds?"

His mother laughed. "You haven't even had firsts yet!"

"So, did you remember any more about the *Northcote*, Mum?" He wanted to know *and* he also wanted to get the conversation as far as possible from cleaning bedrooms.

"The what?" She looked startled. "Oh, that steamboat on the stamp. Hmmm . . . well, I know there was a story about somebody in the family who was on the *Northcote*. I think it was Great-Granny Stark's great uncle who was the captain and he was also one of the pilots — it's called that on a boat when you steer . . . "

"What was his name?" Jeremy interrupted.

"His name? Oh, my goodness, *I* don't remember *that*!" She looked puzzled. "Whatever do you want to know *that* for?"

"Oh, just . . . ummm . . . interested."

"Well, your Aunt Wendy might know. She's got the family tree your grandad put together — I guess you could ask her. Maybe she remembers the story I've forgotten. Why don't you write her a letter? Now," she said, picking up the bowl of spaghetti, "do you still want those seconds?"

Jeremy nodded and held out his plate. "And if she doesn't, she could ask Granny Stark and get the whole story next time she goes to visit her at the nursing home."

His mother sighed. "Jer-Bear, Granny Stark is very sick. I don't think she even knows what's happening right around her a lot of the time."

Now he was sorry he'd brought up the subject. He knew his mum worried a lot about not having gone back to Saskatchewan to visit Granny Stark. Especially now that she was sick. They'd been planning on a trip to Prince Albert last summer, but then the car needed a new transmission and they hadn't gone. At least Aunt Wendy was near enough to visit but that didn't help. Great-Granny was the last family his mother had except for Aunt Wendy — and him, of course. It wasn't all the family Jeremy had, but it might as well have been. He'd been two when his parents divorced, and shortly after that his father remarried and moved away. Now the only contact was an envelope each month addressed to his mother with a cheque in it. Jeremy realized that he wouldn't even recognize his father's handwriting if he did get a letter because the envelopes were always typed. The thought came as something of a surprise. It meant that he really was closer to Great-Granny Stark. At least he knew that spidery writing the minute he saw it.

They finished their spaghetti in silence and Jeremy was helping load the dishwasher when the phone rang. It didn't take him long to see by his mother's face that the news was important . . . and bad.

"Oh no! . . . when did you find out? . . . Yes, I guess I can. . . . Of course, I can . . . are you . . . ?" His mother's voice went on. Jeremy decided it was the most frustrating thing in the world, listening to a conversation like that and not knowing who and what and why. There should be a way to make it illegal not to have both sides of the conversation. But he knew better than to interrupt, so all he could do was listen to the "Oh dear!"s and the "what will we do?"s and run and find a pen because, of course, the one by the phone was dry and wouldn't write the phone number his mother was trying to take down.

Later, watching his mother throw things in her suitcase, he realized that he might have guessed what it was. Of course. It was Aunt Wendy calling because Granny Stark was sicker.

5.

"I'll leave first thing in the morning. If I drive all day I should be in P.A. by suppertime. I should be able to get the time off work. My goodness! What about you? I've got to get somebody to stay with you!" She stopped and reached for the phone by the bed.

Jeremy was stunned. He'd just assumed he was going. "You . . . you mean you're not taking me with you?"

"Oh dear, you know you can't afford to miss any school. Your last report card was bad enough." She looked sympathetic, the way she always did when she felt sorry about punishing him but was going to do it anyway.

"But Mum!" He felt desperate . . . and hopeless.

"I'm sorry! Now run down and get Mrs. Plunkett's phone number for me — maybe she can stay with you." She started folding clothes again.

Jeremy hadn't realized things could get worse. Mrs. Plunkett lived next door and worked as a cleaning lady. Once when his mother was sick and things had got really far behind she'd hired Mrs. Plunkett to come in for a day. It had been one of the blackest days of Jeremy's life. Mrs. Plunkett was nosey, bossy, and she'd thrown out most of his Lego.

The thought of a day with Mrs. Plunkett was unbearable. More than that would kill him for sure. He wanted to throw himself at his mother's feet and beg and plead, but he knew from experience that she would just get tough and say something like, "I'm sorry, dear, but you can't always get your own way, you know."

He walked slowly down the stairs. If only Mrs. Plunkett wasn't home. Well, desperate times call for desperate measures, he'd heard. He carefully copied the phone number down and switched the last two numbers. Now all he had to do was hope that the wrong-number people weren't home.

His mother was making a list when he got back. He set the number down beside the phone without saying anything. Maybe she wouldn't notice . . .

maybe she'd forget. . . . He had to think of something. Anything.

"Mum . . . " he began, but he realized from the look on her face that he was off on the wrong foot. Wrong tone of voice. She hated whining. " . . . ummm . . . can I do anything to help?"

That was better. The expression on her face changed and she smiled gratefully. "Yes. Yes, you can, thank you. Run down to the dryer and bring up the clothes."

When he came back with the laundry basket his mother was on the phone and his heart sank, until he realized she was talking to one of her friends from work.

He started sorting out his own clothes without being asked, stalling for time. He had to think of something, anything, to convince her to take him along.

"You know, Mum," he said, not looking up from the neat piles of socks, "if I was sick I'd have to stay home from school . . . and I haven't missed a single day all year being sick . . . and . . . " He swallowed hard. "I've got a chance to bring up my marks, because we're going to be doing some special projects and I'll work hard . . . really I will. . . . " He had to stop, there was a note of pleading coming into his voice that his mother might decide was whining.

So all he could do was look at her and hope.

It worked! Still, she didn't sound very happy at the idea. "Oh, all right, if you want to so much. Mrs. Plunkett doesn't seem to be answering her phone anyway. I don't understand it . . . there's a light on over there. . . . "

"Thank you, Mum!" He was so relieved, he thought he'd explode. "I'll go get packed."

She laughed a little. "You *are* a funny guy. You're going to be bored out of your skull, you know. All you'll be doing is sitting around, never mind the eight-hour drive. You'd better bring some books to read or something. Oh dear," she said distractedly, "I meant to ask Mrs. Plunkett to pick up the mail. . . . It's funny, I thought I saw her moving around over there. . . . Oh Jeremy, don't forget to pack your toothbrush! Which reminds me, I'd better get mine."

Luckily, she stayed in the bathroom long enough for Jeremy to turn over the note and write the correct phone number on the other side. He laid it beside the phone just the way his mother had left it.

Packing was just a matter of stuffing some clothes into his backpack. The only thing he was careful about was the shabby black stamp book which he placed carefully in a plastic bag, first making sure the *Northcote* stamp was safely inside. With that and the magnifying glass packed he was sure he could think of something to do on the "long, boring drive" tomorrow.

6.

Jeremy knew his mother had got up early and packed a huge box of lunch for the trip. When she'd wakened him, he hadn't felt much like eating but now, sitting in the front seat beside her, he wondered how long he'd have to wait before asking for a sandwich. He supposed at least until they were past the city limits. The lunches his mother packed were one of the things he liked best about taking trips in the car. So he waited, turning every now and then to look in the back at the lunch box, until his mother noticed.

"Either we're being followed or you're hungry!" she teased. "Oh well, you didn't have much breakfast . . . help yourself!"

Jeremy undid his seatbelt and scrambled into

the back seat. Perfect! His mother had thrown some pillows in and, even with his seatbelt on, he could get nice and comfortable. After three sandwiches, he decided this was a wonderful way to spend a day. All that was missing was a little adventure. His mother was busy driving — she would never notice if he took a little boat ride. He laid the stamp album carefully on his lap and picked up the magnifying glass and stamp.

This time it seemed to be early morning; there was still some mist on the river when he arrived on deck. Once again Jeremy enjoyed the scents and sounds of a beautiful spring morning. The clear, sweet notes of a meadowlark drifted down the bank. It felt good to be alive.

And then a shot rang out just as the steamboat was rounding a bend in the river. A signal?

The *Northcote* steamed on. Now he could see a church on the hillside above, scattered houses — and then suddenly gunfire seemed to be coming from everywhere. He jumped as shot ripped and splintered the wooden deck beside him.

He wondered if the bullets would pass through his invisible body, but not enough to stand still and find out. He ducked down, crouching behind the sandbags just as one was hit above him, right where his head had been a minute before. He saw the sacking torn open and not sand but a trickle of grain spilled onto the deck at his feet.

No time to think about that either. A horse with a bearded man in buckskin standing upright in the stirrups pranced back and forth along the bank paying no attention to the rifle fire from the soldiers. The gunmen on the bank of the river were now directing their fire at the little pilot house on the very top of the steamboat.

It was just as the men had said. Some effort had been made to reinforce and protect the bottom half of it, but the top was totally open, so that the man steering could see. As the shot began to strike the flimsy wood around him, Jeremy could see the man make a dive to get out of sight.

As soon as he let go of the wheel the boat veered out of control and scraped against a sandbar. It's going to be wrecked, Jeremy thought. If he could get up to the pilot house he could see what was going on. He crawled across to the steps and scrambled up. Twice there was the splintering of wood as shells struck near him. Once he was sure he felt a puff of air from it striking, it was so close. He was grateful his body was so light and quick. In no time he had scrambled into the pilot house.

Inside, the pilot crouched on the floor, examining a bullet-hole in the sleeve of his jacket as the thin walls of the pilot house were pierced again and again by shells. Another man lay flat. Obviously they would be hit if either of them tried to stand up to steer the boat.

Jeremy grabbed for the wheel. If only he could get control of the wheel and help pull the *Northcote* off the sandbar.

Men were swarming down the bank toward it. They would be boarding the boat soon.

At first Jeremy could barely hold the wheel but then he began to feel it turn, and then the boat was caught in the current and spun loose back into the stream.

He watched as the man on the floor crawled over and seized the wheel, trying to peer at the river, and then quickly ducked down again as the marksmen on shore continued to aim at the wheelhouse.

Over the noise of the shot striking all around was the sound of the shrill tooting of the whistle as the boat moved downstream toward the little settlement on the banks of the river.

"Well, there's Batoche," grumbled the man on the floor. "We're here — where's Middleton and his men?"

"I don't know," said the man crouching by the wheel, "and we'll not wait to see. More steam!" he called.

Jeremy held the wheel. He was beginning to get the feel of it, moving with the steering the pilot was doing. Then he noticed the bearded man in buckskin riding hard towards the ferry landing, shouting orders that Jeremy couldn't hear. But soon men were working frantically on the banks to lower the cable that was strung across the river.

The man beside him with the bullet-torn sleeve saw it too and mumbled under his breath, "Dumont's going to catch us with the ferry cable."

"Full speed ahead!" he yelled and the *Northcote* plowed along trying to beat the descending cable. And all the time the men on either bank of the river kept a steady fire directed at the clumsy steamboat.

The next thing Jeremy knew, they had hit. Down came the two tall spars, the two puffing smokestacks. At last the whistle was silenced as it too fell to the deck.

Coals and cinders fell all around the decks, and some of the soldiers scrambled to scoop up buckets of water to put out the fires that were starting.

For a minute Jeremy thought the cable would hit the pilot house too, but it scraped over the top of it so they could still steer around the bend of the river away from the attack.

7.

It was only after they had gone another kilometre or two and anchored the boat that Jeremy realized that the man in the wheelhouse was Captain Seger. He and the other pilot were having an argument with some of the soldiers who wanted to go back.

"No, Bedson!" the captain was saying. "We'll not go back to Batoche! This is no gunboat. How do you think we'd get past the cable? We'll do our repairs and wait here!"

Jeremy watched as the men began to reset the heavy smokestacks and fix the damaged deck.

He followed two of the soldiers as they helped a third man, who was bleeding from a shoulder wound, into the cabin on the upper deck. Inside, the cabin was even more damaged than the smouldering deck. No fires had started but it was easy to see that this had been the target of much of the attack. Now he understood why those men had been talking about how poorly prepared the cabin was. The thin wooden walls had been no protection against the shot and shell that had bombarded the Northcote. The cabin had been made into a sort of hospital, but when the battle began the sick and wounded had had to take refuge on the floor. Some of them still lay there, their mattresses leaning against the outside walls. There was glass everywhere from the broken skylights, and now that the attack was over the clean-up was beginning. Most attention was going to three men who were bleeding from fresh wounds. Was that all the injured? Jeremy wondered. No one killed? He was surprised at that. There had seemed to be so much gunfire.

When he went back outside there was another argument going on between the army and the crew, but the two men in charge of the *Northcote* did not seem to be backing down a bit.

The officer named Bedson had been joined by another officer who sounded very determined. "We've got to signal our whereabouts to General Middleton. Our orders were to use the whistle." There was an edge to his voice that reminded him of his mother's "Clean up your room and that's an order."

Evidently Captain Seger was not used to taking orders concerning the running of his boat, for he stood his ground. "Well, Captain Smith," was his reply, "if you want the whistle replaced you can send one of your men up to do it. I'm not risking any of my crew. There could be marksmen anywhere on the banks even now."

The army captain turned abruptly and shouted, "Fifty dollars to any man who'll climb that stack and replace the whistle."

It didn't seem like much money to risk your life for. Jeremy was wondering if he could do it. After all, he would be safe. He couldn't be seen to be shot at. He had just started to climb when a young soldier stepped up and began to shinny up the pole.

Now he was in trouble. He would have no trouble staying ahead of the soldier. Jeremy knew he was much faster. But what would happen when he got to the top? There wasn't room for both of them. He was only a couple of metres up, so there was nothing to do but jump — and he did.

The landing would have been all right, but the deck was wet and slippery from the water that had been sluiced around putting out the fires. Jeremy went down, landing hard on his leg. He put out his hand to catch himself. Ouch! He'd cut himself on a sliver of broken glass on the deck. He looked up. Had anybody heard him? Noticed the thud when he'd fallen? No. Luckily they were all concentrating on the young soldier climbing the pole, and there was still the noise of the clean-up going on.

"You men cover Coombs," ordered Bedson, and several guns were aimed in the direction of the nearest shore although Jeremy had seen no movement and assumed that they were far enough away from Batoche to be safe.

He was wrong, for although Coombs had the whistle in place he was still clinging to the stack when a shot rang out, and he only just managed to slide down to safety before another struck the spot where he had been only moments before.

Jeremy stood there squeezing his cut hand. He couldn't even see how big the cut was. But it hurt. That startled him — he wouldn't have thought his invisible body could hurt like that. He remembered the shells that had just missed him when he was climbing to the pilot house and shivered.

It was time to get back. Jeremy realized that he'd spent much longer aboard the *Northcote* than he had intended. What if his mother was trying to talk to him? He hoped that he looked as if he had fallen asleep while looking at the stamp.

He hurried back to the upper deck. Even with his leg a bit sore it *was* wonderful being so light and quick. He wished he felt a bit more like this when he was in his body, but right now he wanted to be back in that heavy, slow body. He found the doorway and once again was curled up in the back seat of the car. Not only did his body feel heavy, it was hot, and he felt like he had a cramp in his leg. He'd just shift a little and get comfortable first. He opened one eye and moved his hand so that he could take a look.

It was a very small cut but it was there. And it was fresh. He stared at the small trickle of blood on the palm of his hand. If it had been a bullet, what then? He didn't like to think about it.

He could see his mother. She was concentrating on driving, singing softly. She always sang on trips. So she hadn't noticed anything. Maybe the thing to do was to pretend he had been asleep. He shut his eyes. It was warm and the steady drone of the motor was soothing. He felt safe.

He woke up to see the sign reading "Prince Albert 45 km" and saw his mother reaching for a sandwich. He yawned and stretched.

"Well! I was beginning to worry about you. I've never seen anybody sit so still and sleep so long. Especially not you." Her voice sounded concerned. "You know, you didn't even wake up when I stopped in Lloydminster for gas and a washroom break." She was looking at him strangely. "You *are* all right, aren't you?"

His mouth was very dry and his left leg felt numb. "I'm okay. Really thirsty, that's all."

She reached over to a bag beside her on the passenger side and handed him a can of pop. "I got you this when I stopped. It's still a *little* bit cold."

The fizzy soft drink felt good on his dry tongue. The trouble was, as soon as he stopped drinking, it made his mouth feel sweet and sticky until he took another sip. He finally gave up — it was only making him thirstier. He sat back and watched the spruce and pine trees whiz by.

"We're almost there. Aunt Wendy will either be at work or with Granny, so there's no point in going to her place." She glanced at her watch. "We made *very* good time, so she wouldn't be expecting us yet. We'll go straight to the nursing home."

8.

Like most of the nursing homes Jeremy had seen in Edmonton, this one was a long, low building. He followed his mother in and sat in the waiting room while she went to the office. It didn't smell like a hospital. There was a mixture of smells, one of which was that kind of disinfectant odour that reminded him of hospitals. The strongest smell was of cooking. But it wasn't the sort that made you hungry. Not the kind that filled the house when his mother was making stew or had a roast in the oven. This was a warm, soggy, cabbagey smell that almost turned his stomach.

His mother came back. "I've found out her room number, but I think you'd better wait here, while I find out how she is . . . if she's . . . well, it might be better if you didn't come in, just in case."

Jeremy looked around the waiting room. Not much to look at. Hardly any furniture, just a few cheap, slightly battered chairs. The only magazines were some tattered *Reader's Digests*. He picked one up. Just as he suspected, it was older than he was. He was bending over to check another one when somebody grabbed him. "How's my favourite nephew?"

Aunt Wendy's perfume knocked the nursing home smell right off the map. It reminded him of laughing and being hugged and, of course, presents. She had always smelled like that, ever since he could remember.

"I didn't think your mother was going to bring you." She shook her finger at him. "Have you finally figured out how to get your way with the woman? I thought you'd never learn!"

He laughed. He always felt like laughing when Aunt Wendy was around, even when nothing funny was happening. She was so full of fun.

"Come on!" She grabbed his hand and led him down the hall. "Granny is having a good day for a change. She even recognized your mum and asked for you!"

"Can you ask her a question?" He knew his mother would want him to sit quietly and not disturb Great-Granny, but if Aunt Wendy asked it would be all right.

"Why don't *you* ask her?"

They were going into the room now. And there was Great-Granny Stark lying on the bed, propped up with pillows, her wispy white hair almost blending in with the pillow case. She looked very much older and more wrinkled than Jeremy remembered her, and her face was pale, a different white from her hair, an old white that had lost its colour. But she was smiling at him.

"I'm so glad you brought the boy, Sandra." Her voice was quivery, like the handwriting had been.

His mother had her hand on his shoulder, pushing him towards the bed. "This is Jeremy," she said in her about-to-cry voice. Jeremy's heart sank. What was he supposed to do now?

Great-Granny's voice got even softer. "You look just like your grandad," she had a remembering look on her face, " . . . just like my Harvey did when he was your age."

Aunt Wendy moved up beside him. "Jeremy has a question for you, Granny," she said and smiled reassuringly at him.

He took a deep breath. "It's about the *Northcote* stamp, Granny, the one you said had some family history about it. . . ."

The old lady looked confused. "Stamp? . . . Family history?" She looked at Aunt Wendy. "What's he talking about, Gwendolyn?"

"Never mind, Granny," his mother said, her voice catching a little. She pulled him back, away from the bed. "Don't bother Granny with your questions now, she's too sick."

"Cool it, Sandy!" Aunt Wendy moved in beside him, pushing his mother out of the way and steering him back to the bed. She leaned over and said softly, "Go ahead, ask again."

He took a deep breath. "I found a stamp . . . in the stamp albums . . . about a steamboat called the *Northcote* . . . and you had written a little note. You said it was about some family history . . . and Mum can't remember the story." He paused, but she still didn't say anything. "Somebody on board the *Northcote*?" he tried again. "It was during the Riel Rebellion?" He was feeling desperate. She didn't remember. "The riverboat . . . at Batoche?"

"Jeremy!" His mother's voice was sharp. "I'm sorry, Granny, he shouldn't . . ."

Jeremy's heart sank. He'd be in trouble now. Probably not even Aunt Wendy could save him from a lecture when he got out of here.

But then Great-Granny started talking.

"Oh, the boat! You're talking about the old

Northcote!" She was smiling at him. "Yes, of course. It was my great-uncle was captain . . . he was one of the pilots too. I never saw the *Northcote*, of course, but my grandmother did. She even got to ride on it."

"During the Rebellion?" Jeremy was beginning to suspect Great-Granny *was* mixed up. There had been no girls on board the *Northcote* all the time he was there.

9.

She didn't seem to be confused but quite alert, and she even laughed at little at that. "No, of course not! The rebellion was just a small part of the *Northcote*'s life. A small part, but a very exciting part. I only saw Great-Uncle John once and I wasn't very old at the time. Maybe not even as old as you are now."

Granny's voice was not loud. It sounded weak, as frail as she looked, as wispy as her hair on the pillow. Aunt Wendy gave him a little shove and he sat carefully on the edge of the bed, leaning closer so as not to miss a word.

"But I remember the day so well," she smiled at Jeremy, her eyes brightening as if she were sharing a secret. "It was because of the ghost, you know!"

"Ghost?" Jeremy couldn't believe it. This was better than he'd ever hoped.

Great-Granny laughed. It wasn't a loud laugh and it wasn't a strong laugh, but it made her look better, gentled the wrinkles and lines of her face somehow.

"It was during the Rebellion, at Batoche . . . of course the pilot house where he was sitting was open on top and so there was no protection, it was right in the line of fire, and he almost got hit by a shell. So he let go of the wheel and the boat ran aground. He was just lying there dodging bullets and shot and suddenly the wheel began to turn by itself. . . . "

"Just started to turn all by itself?" Jeremy asked.

Great-Granny Stark nodded. " . . . and then they were out in the current again and finally managed to get away."

"What about the ghost?" He didn't want her to forget the best part of the story.

"You see, Great-Uncle John was convinced that it wasn't just the current that pulled the Northcote off that sand-bar. He said it was as if somebody was turning the wheel. And I suppose it made a big impression on him because it saved his life."

This was news to Jeremy. "The ghost *really* saved his life?"

"No sitting on the bed, young man!" a brittle voice behind him said. A woman in a pink uniform had come in without Jeremy noticing.

Great-Granny ignored her and kept talking to Jeremy, even though he was now off the bed, standing close to Aunt Wendy. "You see, if the *Northcote* had stayed stuck a minute longer, when they lowered the ferry cable at Batoche, it would have gone right through the wheelhouse he was in and he would have been killed!"

Jeremy hadn't thought of that. He wanted to cheer, but he just stood there with a big smile on his face.

"It's time for our medication, Mrs. Stark," said the pushy voice as the woman moved between them and the bed. "Enough talking for now. We mustn't tire ourselves must we?"

"Mrs. Grimshaw! My sister has driven all the way from Edmonton to see our grandmother. We are entitled to visit her." It was a voice Jeremy didn't recognize, steel-coated with icicles dripping from it. He actually had to turn to see who it was coming from. He had never heard Aunt Wendy sound so angry.

As usual, it was his mother who tried to smooth

things out. "It's all right, we'll just say good-bye and come back this evening." She went forward to kiss Granny lightly on the forehead.

Granny was still ignoring the woman and smiling straight at Jeremy as Aunt Wendy pushed him forward again.

"Thank you for the family story, Great-Granny," he said. He felt like giving her a bear hug, but he was afraid to. She looked so thin and frail, as if she'd break if he did. So he kissed her soft white cheek instead.

"Thank you for coming." She smiled, but her voice did sound tired. "You've done me more good than all of Grimshaw's pills."

"Sometimes I wish that Grimshaw creature would choke on her share of 'our' medication!" Aunt Wendy complained as they walked out of the nursing home into the fresh air. "But," her voice brightened as she patted Jeremy on the back, "this guy really did Granny a world of good. I haven't seen her so 'with it' for weeks. It's a darn good thing you brought him along, Sandy," she said, giving Jeremy a big wink.

His mother looked doubtful. "She certainly doesn't seem as bad as you thought. But I'm so glad we came. I've been meaning to the last couple of years, but I just kept putting it off, or something would come up. I just wish we could stay, but I'm missing work and Jeremy's missing school."

"Well, you visit her tonight and leave the kid to me," Aunt Wendy grinned at him. "We'll dine out — I know a great hamburger joint. Just the place for a classy couple like us!"

It was a wonderful thought. Jeremy realized he was starving.

10.

They visited Great-Granny Stark the next morning before starting back to Edmonton but the visit was not the same. His mother said Granny had slept all through her visit the evening before. And she might as well have now. She obviously didn't know who any of them were. Jeremy thought she didn't even *see* them. He stood beside the bed feeling sad and awkward. He could hear his mother sniffling behind him. Aunt Wendy's efforts to get the old woman's attention failed every time.

Granny Stark's fingers moved constantly, plucking at the bedclothes as she mumbled words they couldn't understand. It made Jeremy feel sad, because she was obviously trying to talk to them, but even Aunt Wendy couldn't figure out what she was trying to say.

She sighed. "We might as well go. This is how it usually is when she's awake. Yesterday was just a good day, I guess."

They were saying good-bye when Great-Granny seemed to rouse herself. He almost thought she was going to recognize him and talk to him again, because she stopped fumbling with the sheet and held his arm. "You're spending too much time with those stamps . . . " she said, " . . . all day you're in the room with that magnifying glass and those stamps. . . . "

That startled them all. Jeremy was amazed. How did she know how much time he spent with the stamps?

His mother started to answer, "It's just the last few days . . . I'm sure it's not . . . "

The old lady interrupted. "You should get outside more, Harvey. You're getting quite peaked."

She thinks I'm Grandad, Jeremy realized. She thinks it's years ago and I'm her boy! He could hear his mother's sharp intake of breath as she understood it too.

"Now run along and get some fresh air . . . " the quivery voice was hard to hear. "Hours and hours just sitting there with those stamps . . . holding your magnifying glass . . . never moving. Such a boy!" She was smiling now, her eyes shut, happily remembering her own child. "Run along, Harvey," she said. And then she slept.

Walking to the car in the bright sunshine, Jeremy didn't listen to what his mother and Aunt Wendy were saying. He was thinking about the stamps. Grandad's stamps. Grandad as a boy his age, sitting with the magnifying glass for "hours and hours."

At first when they started the drive back to Edmonton he sat in the front seat, even though he really wanted to be in the back seat with his backpack and the stamp book. His mother was very quiet — unhappy, he supposed, at leaving. Maybe he could talk to her and cheer her up a little.

"I'm glad you brought me," he said. "It was really interesting finding out that Captain Seger was my great-great — how many greats would that be, Mum?"

It seemed to work. She was looking interested and not so sad.

"Hmmm . . . let's see. He was *your* Great-Granny's great-uncle . . . so that's *one* great to start with, then there would be *another* great to go with her parents and . . . *one* for the great in great-granny . . . " She was holding up fingers, one for every great. "You do understand that 'great' just means another generation, don't you?"

He didn't. And he didn't much care either. He'd managed to take his mother's mind off feeling sad. She was intent on this explanation. He was obviously going to get a lesson on 'great'-ness whether he wanted it or not.

"For example, when you have children, your Aunt Wendy will be their Great-Aunt Wendy. I'll just be Grandma, but when your children have children, I'll be Great-Grandma and she'll be their great-*great*-aunt." She looked at him proudly. "Got that?"

He nodded, "I think so." He was glad there wasn't going to be a test on this later.

"So," she said, "we've got *three* greats. And then *one* for Grandad's generation and *one* for mine." She held up five fingers and said triumphantly, "which makes him your Great-great-great-great-great-Uncle John. Jeremy," she said in a different tone of voice, "what did you say his last name was?"

"Seger," said Jeremy, and then he realized his mother was looking at him very strangely.

"I don't remember," she said, sounding puzzled, "Granny calling him anything but Great-Uncle John. . . . "

Uh, oh, Jeremy thought. Think fast. "Ummmm, she didn't? Well . . . I guess maybe Aunt Wendy told me when we were talking last night while you were out."

She seemed to accept that. Jeremy started to relax. He *had* talked about it to Aunt Wendy last night. She'd wanted to know how he knew so much about the Rebellion and about Batoche. He'd said his mother had told him. He was really lucky they hadn't both asked him at the same time. He'd have to be more careful in the future.

"I think I'll just climb in the back seat now . . . with that lunch Aunt Wendy packed." He'd seen her do it; fried chicken and dill pickles and lots of other great things. He was *very* hungry.

They were already past Shellbrook before he settled back and took out the album. It took him a few minutes to discover that the *Northcote* stamp was missing.

"Mum! It's gone! The *Northcote* stamp's gone!" He felt a terrible panic. He had found a magic stamp and just when he was learning about it, he'd lost it.

"Oh," said his mother in an annoyingly calm voice, "I forgot to tell you. I lent it to Aunt Wendy. She was very interested after yesterday and wanted to look at it. I knew you'd already examined it so I thought you wouldn't mind."

Mind? Wouldn't mind? He wanted to scream, "Turn this car around and go back, right now," but he didn't dare. He just sat there feeling a great lumpy sad feeling.

"I lent her your magnifying glass too. Did she remember to put it back?" His mother was more concerned with adjusting the sun visor. "Never mind, I'll lend you mine, when we get home."

The magnifying glass too! Jeremy dug frantically through the backpack, but he knew right away that Aunt Wendy hadn't remembered to put it back. For the first time in his life, he didn't like Aunt Wendy very much. How could she do this to him?

He turned the pages of the album slowly, but without the magnifying glass he couldn't see the details very well and nothing moved. It was going to be a very long trip home.

11.

It was late when they got home. He was feeling sad and sulky even though his mother had agreed to stop in Vegreville for pizza.

"So where's this magnifying glass I can use?" he grumbled, throwing his backpack down in the hallway. He wasn't tired and maybe, just maybe, the *Northcote* wasn't the only stamp that worked.

"Glass? Oh yes, I did promise you could use it." She was in the kitchen putting away the milk and bread they'd picked up for tomorrow. "I think it's on my desk."

Jeremy grabbed his pack and started up the stairs.

"You know," said his mother, following him, "I thought it was *my* magnifying glass you were using until Wendy noticed the initials scratched on it. H.I.S. — Harvey Ian Stark. You dug it out of one of the boxes didn't you?" They were in front of his bedroom now and she gave his shoulder a little squeeze goodnight. "Did you know it was Grandad's?"

He shook his head. No. And yet, maybe somehow he had. Now, as he sat in bed with the album, even before he raised the magnifying glass to his eye, he knew it wouldn't work. Somehow he wasn't disappointed. "Hours and hours just sitting there with those stamps . . . holding your magnifying glass. . . . " Granny Stark had said. It wasn't the *Northcote* stamp that was special, he knew now. It was the magnifying glass. Grandad's magnifying glass he'd had as a boy. Jeremy had to get it back.

The minute his mother left for work in the morning, he phoned Aunt Wendy. He knew how to do it. The number "1" for long distance and then the area code and Aunt Wendy's number written by the phone. It was an emergency number for him. He knew he shouldn't use it without permission but this was an emergency. If only Aunt Wendy hadn't left for work yet . . .

"Hi kiddo!" she said, when she found out who it was. "You just caught me going out the door. What's up?"

"I *need* my magnifying glass . . . Grandad's magnifying glass. Mum said she lent it to you and you forgot to put it back. Can you send it. Soon?" Even if she mailed it right away he probably wouldn't get it for a week.

"Not to worry, Amigo! You've got it!"

Jeremy couldn't understand what she meant. "It's not in my backpack."

"No, you'd already put your pack in the car so I stuck it in your mum's suitcase — in the zipper pocket thing on the side. Honest! I was going to put it in the food bag but I was afraid your mother, Tidy Tillie, wouldn't notice it and chuck the lunch remains in the garbage." She laughed. "That is, if there were any remains with *you* around! Listen! Can't talk now. . . . I'm going to be late for work!"

"Thanks, Aunt Wendy," he said. "You are . . . " but all he could hear was the buzz. She was gone. He felt sorry he'd been so mad at her yesterday, but most of all he felt relieved and very, very happy.

It was time to go to school now, but the minute he got home he'd get the magnifying glass out.

He had to run the last two blocks to school and even at that he was almost late. But he didn't care. He spent the day thinking about that other ship stamp he'd noticed.

The *Nonsuch* was an interesting looking ship.

Sixteen sixty-eight, it had said on the stamp. Was there a door on the deck? He could hardly wait to get home and look at it with the magnifying glass.

12.

Jeremy sat at his desk with the stamp album. He had both magnifying glasses. He tried his mother's first. The *Nonsuch* was beautiful. The way the sails billowed and the waves tossed was exciting. But his heart sank a little as he examined the stamp. He couldn't see a door. How would he get on board?

He had to admit that he was having doubts now. All day, he'd believed it would work. Believed that Grandad's magnifying glass would make it work. But now that he was about to try it he was afraid. There was this feeling nibbling away inside that maybe it was just the *Northcote*, just the one stamp that had the power. . . .

He picked up the old magnifying glass and

looked at it. It was pretty scratched up all right and there were the H.I.S. initials.

"Hours and hours," Great-Granny had said. He took a deep breath and held it to his eye. At first the *Nonsuch* looked just the way it had with the other magnifying glass but then there was something . . . some movement. The sail billowed. No. More than that . . . it flapped! And when it did, he could see the cabin door.

Next thing he knew he was in the doorway on the old sailing ship. He was on board the *Nonsuch*!

His feeling of elation died very quickly. It seemed as if the world was tossing about like a wild bronco. He was conscious of wind and waves, waves that lifted and tossed the ship as if it were a toy.

But Jeremy's first problem was the wind. In his present lighter body he felt himself being blown over the side of the ship and only managed to throw his arms around something as he went. His eyes were shut against the spray. Then, as the ship mounted a mountainous wave, he opened one eye just a crack. He was so surprised he almost lost his grip on the dog.

Dog? It was a carved dog. Lying there on the ship's railing, paws crossed as if guarding the way like stone lions do on the steps of old buildings. A hunting dog or hound, the kind you sometimes saw in old paintings with a pile of dead birds nearby. Jeremy couldn't remember ever seeing dogs on ships before — mermaids and lady figureheads, but dogs?

He held on tight. He didn't want to think about what would happen if he was blown overboard. If glass could cut you, then bullets could kill you or waves could drown you. He shut his eyes and hung on with all his might.

The waves slamming against the ship were not only cold — they were strong. He realized he could be washed overboard at any minute. He'd better get inside. He'd been coming through that doorway when he got here. Now he had to try to get back to it.

He began to ease himself over the dog, straddling it for a minute, still desperately holding onto its neck as he lowered himself to the deck.

"I'm sure glad you were here, boy," he whispered in its ear as he reached for the next handhold.

It was all he could do to hold on to the rope he'd grabbed, for just then the ship give a mighty lurch and the next wave washed right over the deck below him.

Two men were working the pump just in front of him, turning it round and round like a giant corkscrew, pumping away the water that continually collected on the deck. Actually there were men everywhere, swarming around the decks. It looked crowded in the small space, but everybody seemed to have a job and they weren't getting in each other's way. Most of them were hauling on the ropes. There were ropes everywhere, hundreds of ropes going up to the sails and up the high mast.

He looked up, squinting into the storm. The mast towered far above. He couldn't imagine how the ship didn't tip over with all that height. He couldn't see very well but it didn't look to be very long. Not nearly as long as it was high.

Not far from him the sailors were shouting. Something about the "mizzenmast." He wished he could hear better, but the storm made so much noise. He'd never heard anything so loud — a big sound that filled his ears. The relentless pounding of the waves was loud and constant, and through it he could hear the shrieking wind in the shrouded sails above him.

It was wonderful the way the crew moved on the deck. Here he was, barely able to hang on, he couldn't even imagine walking and yet they were *working*. Moving about, crab-like, from place to place, but sure-footed on the slippery deck, even as the ship rose and fell with the waves.

He clung to the ropes, wondering if he could

reach the doorway the next time the waves let up a little. Just then the ship rose on a giant wave and seemed to pause, suspended, and then it dropped with a sickening plunge. Jeremy felt his stomach lurch. This was worse than any roller coaster ride. He had to get to the doorway. There! He made it! He hung on for a minute then, as a great wave of spray hit him, he backed through.

13.

And was sitting at his desk again. Darn! He hadn't meant to come back yet. Except sitting here, back in his real body, he wasn't too sorry. Especially since his mother was in the bedroom doorway. He wondered how long she'd been standing there.

" . . . and I *told* you to put that shirt in the wash! Just because I'm gone to work by the time you head for school doesn't mean you can slouch off looking neglected. You *do* have other shirts, you know."

Jeremy sighed. He did, of course. But this one was special. Aunt Wendy had brought this one back from California. It was neon green with a skateboarder on the front doing an ollie, and the first time he'd worn it a couple of junior high guys at the bus stop had said, "Nice shirt, kid! Where'd you get it?" and his friend Charlie had said, "Wow! Cool shirt, dude!" And besides it was loose and comfortable, although his mother said it was too big and Aunt Wendy should learn his size. Anyway, it wasn't *that* dirty, even though he'd worn it three days — or was it four? He'd tried very hard to keep it clean. So what if there *was* a bit of ketchup here and there and the odd smudge? He thought he'd done very well.

Anyway he didn't feel like arguing all that much. He felt kind of queasy. Like his stomach was still flipping around somewhere on the *Nonsuch*.

" . . . and, furthermore, I know you were too tired to take a bath last night, but you'd better not forget tonight. How long since you . . . ?"

Jeremy put his hand over his mouth and made a dash past his mother for the bathroom. He didn't even dare open his mouth to yell "Gangway!"

"Jeremy! What's the matter, honey?" She was right behind him now. When he finished, she handed him a washcloth.

"Thanks, Mum." He wiped his mouth, ran a glass of water and swished it around, rinsing his mouth. The room seemed to be spinning a bit but at least the sink was something solid to hang onto.

"Oh dear! It's that 'flu. Everybody's been getting it. Would you like a glass of ginger ale?"

Jeremy nodded. Actually, he was feeling quite a bit better already. But he thought he'd just stay here a minute, in case.

His mother was already out the door on her way to the kitchen.

"Into bed as soon as you can. And no school for you tomorrow."

She always said it that way. As if staying home from school was some kind of punishment. Of course she claimed that when she was young she'd just hated to miss school. Jeremy sighed.

It was tough having a mother who'd never been a normal kid. She didn't understand things. Like the shirt. It wasn't *very* dirty — you could still see most of the picture and some of the writing. His mother was some kind of laundry fanatic, that was all.

He made his way back to his room. He realized he'd never really appreciated the stillness of houses before. Nice the way they didn't move about the way ships did. And his bed looked so peaceful, just standing there, not bobbing around. Oh, oh, he shouldn't think of bobbing around, he was starting to feel queasy again. He lay down and shut his eyes. No, not a good thing, that seemed to make the room move again. And now it felt like his bed was spinning around with him on it. He opened his eyes and the spinning stopped.

"Here's some ginger ale and crackers." His mother put the glass on the bedside table and handed him a plate.

"Crackers?" He looked at them doubtfully.

"Well, they're *supposed* to settle the stomach. Although I don't think there's much you can do about the 'flu. Everybody says it's a bad one. You'll probably have to stay home from school for several days." She was looking at him with sympathy again, as if this was going to be a hardship or something.

"Just when you've already missed two days for the trip. I'm so sorry."

"I'll try to be brave!" he said, trying not to smile and look too cheerful. He couldn't very well tell her he didn't have the 'flu after all, could he? She'd never believe it if he said he was seasick.

"You know it's almost time for bed anyway. You might as well get undressed. And," she said, as she left his room, "*put that shirt in the clothes hamper!*"

"Sure, Mum." No problem. By the time he had to go back to school he could wear it again.

He still felt a bit woozy as he undressed. He picked up the stamp book and magnifying glass and set it on the bedside table. It wasn't hard to resist the temptation to focus the glass on the *Nonsuch*. He just had to think about that wild, tossing ship to convince himself that he would be better off to wait until morning. Maybe the storm would be over by then.

It seemed to be a long night. He dreamed he was alone in the ocean tossed about by mountainous waves, and just as the waves were closing over his head and he was sinking, a beautiful dog would grab his shirt in its teeth and pull him up. But when he turned to hold onto it, it was made of wood. Just a carved wooden dog floating in the water.

When he woke up it was late and the sun was shining in the window. He sat up. Not dizzy — in fact he felt pretty good. Except for his mouth, which felt terrible. It felt as if some furry creature had crawled in there and died.

For once, he thought, as he headed for the bathroom, he was really looking forward to brushing his teeth, not just wetting his toothbrush so his mother would think he had.

14.

There was a note from his mother propped on the dresser.

"Dear Jeremy," it said. "I hope you're feeling better. You were sleeping so soundly I decided not to wake you when I left for work. I'll come home at lunch-time and see how you are. Any problems, phone me at work, or if it's an emergency call Mrs. Plunkett."

Not Mrs. Plunkett! Jeremy tried to imagine an emergency that would force him to call Mrs. Plunkett.

Fire? No. He'd call the fire department and then clean up the mess himself. Uzi-toting terrorists carrying him off to be locked up in some dark dingy hideout? No! He'd go quietly so long as they didn't kidnap Mrs. Plunkett and put her in the same closet. Monsters from outer space? No! Maybe he could persuade them to take Mrs. Plunkett for their fiendish purposes instead. Lions and tigers and bears? Eat me, guys, better than being with Mrs. Plunkett any time.

"Lions and tigers and bears . . . lions and tigers and bears," he chanted as he walked briskly to the kitchen. He felt great!

The toast popped and he decided that he was really very hungry. Mum had said "Eat toast," but just to make it interesting he put on some peanut butter, and then some jelly, and then a few slices of apple, and then some cheese slices. It was one of his finest creations.

It took him quite a while to clean up the kitchen. He left a few toast crumbs and a buttery knife on the counter so his mother would believe he'd eaten the toast, but everything else he put away. If his mother realized he wasn't sick he'd be back to school that very afternoon.

Back in bed, propped up with pillows, he set the stamp book on his lap and picked up the magnifying glass. Better be ready to grab something in case that storm's still blowing, he thought.

It wasn't stormy, but the waves were still swelling pretty high. High enough to make the ship rise and fall more than he liked, but without the wind he could move around quite nicely. The sun was shining and the air had a crisp ocean tang. It was beautiful, nothing but sky and sea all around him — and the ship, of course. Now he could explore the ship.

On the deck above him a couple of men stood smoking pipes. Other men below him worked at various jobs. One rough-looking man was clearing away torn canvas that was plugging the holes along the deck so that the water the others were pumping up could run overboard.

"When ye've finished clearing the scuppers, Perkins, go and help mend the spritzle," someone over his head called.

Jeremy looked up. High on the mast, legs wrapped around the cross bars that held the sails, a man was perched fixing something. As he looked, he realized there were others doing the same thing. They reminded him of big birds sitting on perches. It made him dizzy just looking at them.

He let go of the doorway he'd grabbed when he first arrived and walked carefully past the man at the pump. He followed the other man — it must be Perkins — who was walking toward the lower deck. Perkins was supposed to mend the "spritzle," whatever that was.

It turned out to be a sail that hung straight out from the front of the ship, almost in the water. Jeremy realized the man must have been saying "sprit*sail*." This sailor-talk was going to be hard to understand.

The "spritzle" must have been in the water during the storm, for the canvas was badly torn. A man was working with a needle and thread and Perkins was soon doing the same. Jeremy watched for a minute or two, admiring the deft way the men sewed, neatly turning the frayed bits and patching the sail, their needles moving quickly through the heavy material.

He decided to go below deck, into the hold, and see what was there. The crew must sleep somewhere and there was bound to be cargo. It would be interesting to see what this ship carried.

15.

When his eyes got used to the darkness down below, Jeremy realized that he was in the crew's quarters. Squeezed against the sides of the ship there were bunks, low and narrow. Nothing like any bunk bed he had ever seen, more like boxes — or coffins. They couldn't possibly sleep there.

But they did, because two of the sailors *were* sleeping right now and there were two more along the wall ahead. Jeremy realized that, aside from being narrow and cramped, the bunks were short. Now that he thought about it, most of the sailors on deck hadn't been much taller than he was. Although they looked shorter because of the funny, rolling side-to-side walk they had. That way of walking made them move so easily and not lose balance with the tossing of the ship. But surely some of them must be taller. What did they do? He heard a noise and there blocking the narrow passage in front of him was probably the answer: a man sleeping in a hammock. Well, if he had to sleep down here that would probably be best, Jeremy thought. Swaying with the motion of the ship would be nice, sort of like rock-a-bye-baby. He looked at the bearded, wind-beaten face of the sailor snoring loudly in front of him. Some baby!

But even without the cramped coffin-like bunk Jeremy knew he could never stand sleeping down here. The smell was terrible! He'd have to get back on deck for some fresh air pretty soon.

A movement on the floor near one of the bunks attracted his attention. A rat as big as Mrs. Plunkett's cat, Horatio, lurked in the shadows. Its eyes seemed to gleam red in the partial light as it moved towards Jeremy's feet.

In an instant Jeremy was on deck. It was a good thing there'd been nobody on the ladder when he'd scrambled up and through the hatch. He could really move this invisible body when he had to.

By the time he finished exploring the ship, he'd learned a bit more about the crew and just how crowded twelve men would be on this ship. He wondered how long they'd been at sea and how much longer they would have to be. Imagine sleeping in those awful box-like bunks night after night. He'd discovered something when he counted the crew and then, braving the rats, went below to count the bunks. There were four more on the other side which made eight bunks. They obviously took turns using them. Jeremy guessed that made sense since some of them would be on deck at night. And, as he'd seen, some of the men used hammocks. He supposed you could set one up anywhere. He knew where he'd set his if he was sleeping on this ship. On deck in the fresh air, that's where.

So they didn't even have their own bunks, no corner to call their own. As far as he could see, no place to store things either. Where did they keep their clothes?

Not that their clothes were much to look at. Baggy pants with tar all over, so that it was hard to tell what colour the heavy, rough material had been to begin with. Heavy checked shirts, blue and white — although again the colour was dimmed by grime. (Obviously these guys had no mothers tearing the shirts off their backs to wash.)

He'd found out something else too. After he'd seen one of the sailors leaning over the side of the ship, he'd checked below deck again. There was no bathroom. Nothing. Which, of course, meant no baths either. Sailors *obviously* didn't have mothers!

No baths and no changes of clothes. It could be wonderful. Except . . . it did smell *awful* below decks. Probably would smell terrible *on* deck too, if it weren't in the open air. And he had to admit there were times when a bath was nice. He'd bet even these guys would have liked a nice tub of warm water to soak in after spending several hours being drenched in cold salt water during last night's storm. You'd think with all this water . . . Jeremy realized that was it! It was *salt* water. You wouldn't want to wash in *salt* water. And fresh water would be precious. You'd have to bring it with you and keep it just for drinking. He realized that he'd seen the men going to a keg for a drink, and it wasn't water they were drinking. It was beer!

In his exploration he'd left the cabin for last. This was the doorway he'd come through. He wasn't quite sure if he could go through it without ending up back home. Now it didn't matter. It was time to get back, in case his mother came home for lunch early.

He was sitting in bed trying to look sick when his mother came in.

"Oh good!" she said, "you look *much* better!" Luckily she interpreted his look of disappointment as a spasm of pain, for she suddenly became sympathetic. "I feel so awful leaving you alone like this, when you're sick, but I just couldn't take any more time off from work right now, in case I have to go back to see Granny again. Are you *sure* you don't want me to ask Mrs. Plunkett . . . ?"

"No!" Jeremy almost shouted. "No." He tried to sound calm and mature, the way a person who didn't need a babysitter would sound, although the threat of Mrs. Plunkett's company made him want to howl and holler like a baby.

16.

The little bowl of soup, with more crackers for his "upset" stomach, made him very glad he'd had a substantial breakfast.

He could hardly wait for his mother to leave so he could fix himself another snack.

That reminded him. He hadn't noticed the men on board the ship eating. What did they eat? he wondered. Maybe he'd catch them at it next time he went on the ship. He didn't think they'd be lucky enough to have peanut butter and jelly.

"Jeremy," his mother called as she was getting on her coat. "I'm going to call at the school and tell Mrs. Das why you're away and pick up any assignments you need to be doing."

"Gee, thanks Mum," he said under his breath.

She came into his room to kiss him good-bye. "Do you want anything?"

He wasn't quite sure how to ask. "Ummm . . . well, could you maybe get me some information about that ship? The *Nonsuch*, it's called . . . the one that stamp's about . . . " Oh boy, his mother was really looking at him strangely. "Just curious . . . ummm . . . you know . . . "

"Sure, I guess so. Sorry to look so puzzled. That's not your usual request, you know," she laughed. "Usually it's food!"

He waited for several minutes after she'd left. It wouldn't do for her to come back and catch him in the kitchen making a sandwich when she'd just given him lunch.

Sixteen sixty-eight, the stamp said. That was a long time ago, Jeremy thought, three hundred and . . . twenty . . . whatever. Math wasn't his best subject. Anyway it *was* a long time ago.

The flag on the front of the ship was different too, just a plain red cross on a white background. Not the Union Jack. The stamp didn't tell him *anything* about the ship except that it was very, very old. And yet, he thought, as he climbed out of bed, he probably knew more about it than most people. After all, he'd been on board and seen those olden days sailors at work.

Two sandwiches later, he felt *much* better. The nice part was that he had a whole afternoon to himself and somewhere interesting to go that didn't depend on somebody else driving him or giving him permission, and what's more, it didn't cost him a thing!

For all that, he sat in bed with the stamp book on his lap for a few minutes, savouring the feeling of expectation. It was sort of like Christmas morning, taking a few minutes between going through your stocking presents and starting on your under-the-tree presents. Last year he'd even eaten a few pieces of the orange that had been in his stocking before his curiosity about the big lumpy parcel from Aunt Wendy got the better of him. He was beginning to feel that way again. He picked up the magnifying glass.

There was great excitement aboard the ship. Gulls and other sea birds wheeled and turned in the sky filling the air with their cries. Jeremy realized that he hadn't seen any the other two times he'd been on board. Everyone, except the man holding the big steering rudder on the upper deck behind him, was crowded near the front, pointing.

In the distance, a dark line against the horizon. Was that why everyone was so excited?

Last time he'd been on board he'd tried to figure

out which men were officers and which were the lowly sailors. It wasn't easy. After all they weren't wearing uniforms or the kind of caps he'd always associated with sailors, little round ones for the men and brimmed ones for the officers. He figured out the captain soon enough. The sturdy-looking man giving orders and being called "Cap'n." There were two other men giving orders and two more who were obviously not sailors. One of them, an older man, was now standing nearby in close conversation with the captain.

Being invisible should have been perfect for eavesdropping. But Jeremy had trouble figuring out what was being said. Bad enough that he didn't know anything about the different sails and masts and parts of the ship, but they all talked with such strange accents. The older man, for instance, and his friend spoke French together, but even the crew, who spoke English, talked with different dialects and with all the noises of the ship, Jeremy had to admit he lost most of the conversations.

"By my reckoning that land's the Terra La Bradore, m'sieu Gooseberries," the captain was saying. "We've sailed more'n five hundred leagues since Gravesend. Forty-eight days since we set our course westerly off the Fair Isle. "

Jeremy moved closer. There was a brisk wind

that threatened to blow him overboard, and the noise of the seabirds almost drowned out what the captain was saying.

"Bon! Capitaine Gillam. We find the passage, but first we sail to find the furs on the great Bay of the North." This man, the older man, looked strong and tough, but Jeremy was sure, by the awkward way he moved about on deck, that he was the one person there who was not at home on board ship. He looked as if he'd had a rough life, and his weatherbeaten features showed that he was used to the outdoors. But he looked very different from the sailors and the captain.

"Yaaar, please the prince and company," the captain replied, "and then . . . "

But just then the man at the tiller called something about a "course west norwest!" and the captain left.

17.

"Romieux," the older man called, and once more he and his friend began a conversation in French.

Jeremy had spent two years in immersion classes, but then his mother couldn't afford to keep the house any more, and after the move to a new school he'd got so far behind he persuaded his mother to let him take regular classes. He could understand a bit of what the men were saying, but like the English, it seemed to be full of words and phrases he couldn't figure out. And the accent was so different, he soon gave up and drifted away. All he'd managed to make out was that they were talking about the older man's brother, "Pierre," and Trois-Rivières. And he was called, not "Gooseberries," but "Médar" by the other man. Maybe he'd find out the right name if his mother found a book for him.

Just then there was a shout from below deck and one of the men — it looked like Perkins — came up with a handful of hard-looking biscuits and a piece of meat in his other hand. One by one those men who weren't working went below and came back carrying food.

No plates, no vegetables (sailors definitely didn't have mothers), just the hard-looking meat and the even harder-looking chunks of biscuit. Well, he'd been curious about what they ate, but he was glad he didn't have to eat it even though he wondered what it tasted like. He supposed the meat was salted. He'd heard that was how they'd kept things from spoiling in the days before refrigerators. Somewhere he'd even heard that they carried cows and sheep on the ship to have fresh meat, but there was no room on this boat for any animal. Other than the rats, of course.

"Fish!" a man aloft in the rigging called. "Cod — and big 'uns!" There was movement and excitement again, and Jeremy watched with admiration as the man on the rigging scrambled down, agile as a monkey.

Perkins had disappeared into the hold at the first call. Now he was back carrying a net, and without a word the two men dropped it over the side away from the direction the ship was moving.

The face of the sailor next to Jeremy broke into a broad grin and he tucked away the biscuit he'd been gnawing. "Stow the hardtack . . . there'll be fish!"

The weathered face reminded him of one of those dolls you make out of apples. The kind you carve and then leave and, as the apple turns brown and shrivels, it looks like an old, old face.

Added to that, this man looked as if his nose had been broken one too many times. Not a pretty sight. But that wasn't the worst of it. Maybe an apple face with its wrinkles and creases was supposed to give the doll character. And maybe this battered seaman would be an interesting study for some photographer, except that Jeremy knew cameras hadn't been invented yet. But it wouldn't be a good idea to smile for the camera because the grinning sailor had the most disgusting-looking set of teeth he'd ever seen. That is, what teeth he *had* were the worst. There were more missing than were there. The ones he had left were blackened and some appeared to be just stumps. He'd bet this guy could write a book about toothache. No wonder he was smiling at the thought of some fresh fish for his next meal. He must have a terrible time chewing the salted meat and "hardtack" with *that* set of choppers. Jeremy decided, now that he'd seen the grin, that the man didn't look like an apple-face doll at all, more like a very badly carved Jack-o'-lantern a week after Hallowe'en.

He noticed that the man hadn't thrown the biscuit overboard, though. Didn't he believe they'd catch any fish? Maybe, Jeremy mused, even bad food was precious on a voyage like this where you wouldn't know how long it would take but there was room for only so much food.

He needn't have worried about the fishing. Perkins and the other sailor were pulling in the net, and there were smiles on the faces of all the crew. The sight would be enough to keep a dentist busy for years. It surprised Jeremy that even the younger men had many gaps in their mouths. What happened to their teeth?

The deck near Perkins seemed to be alive with the flopping, glistening fish. Now Perkins had his knife out and was grabbing those nearest him and quickly cutting off their heads and gutting them. Jack-o'-lantern had gone below and brought back a large iron pot which was soon half full of the pieces of fish.

Perkins had a lot of help, for any man who wasn't working or eating had produced a sharp knife. Heads and tailfins and all the other bits were being thrown overboard to the delight of the screaming, diving gulls that now followed the ship. Soon all that was left of the mass of flopping fish was the pieces in the pot and a few bloody bits on the deck. Jacko had grabbed a bucket, dipped it full of sea water and was sloshing water on the deck, sending the small bits of fin and blood overboard through the scuppers. Jeremy noticed one small fish that seemed to have managed to avoid the slaughter. It had flopped over behind some ropes and now a swoosh of water carried it through the scupper.

Aha! Jeremy thought, feeling happy for the fish. A survivor makes his getaway! Even though he knew the sailors deserved a break from the dry, salted food they'd had to eat he couldn't help feeling a bit of sympathy for the fish. He moved over so he could see it fall safely back into its ocean home.

But just as the gleaming sliver of silver hit the water a big gull swooped down, and all that Jeremy could see was a bit of tailfin sticking out of the gull's bill as it flew away again.

Jacko took the pot full of fish below and soon the aroma of chowder came wafting up. Even to Jeremy's modern nose it smelled pretty good. It reminded him that he'd better get home, since his mother would be getting back soon.

As he backed through the doorway, one of the men began singing and soon the others joined in:

Ye gentlemen of England
that live at home at ease
Full little do ye think upon
the dangers of the seas
Give ear unto the mariners
for they will plainly show
The cares and fear when
the stormy winds do blow.

18.

Jeremy was waiting impatiently when his mother came into his room.

"I got . . . " she began.

"Did you get a book?" he interrupted.

She began to laugh. "I was going to say I got a pizza!" she said. "I forgot food's not the top of your list of priorities anymore."

"Pizza? Great!" He was starved.

"So you're feeling better? I was afraid it might be too soon for pizza." She looked concerned. "I can make you soup instead."

Rats, he'd almost blown it. It wouldn't do to get too well, too soon. "No . . . " he tried to make his voice sound unenthusiastic, a bit doubtful, "no, I think I can handle a pizza." He hoped she'd brought a big one.

"I was going to phone but then I thought you might be sleeping."

Oh, oh, Jeremy thought. That was close. If she'd phoned and he hadn't answered she'd have panicked and goodness knows what she'd have done. The police? Mrs. Plunkett? An awful thought.

"I'm glad you didn't . . . I sorta . . . dozed off . . . might not have heard the phone."

She was doing her mother-of-sick-boy routine now, plumping pillows, straightening the bed, putting the stamp book and magnifying glass away, and generally messing things up just when he had everything where he wanted them. "I'm glad you had a nap. You *are* feeling better aren't you? No more upset stomach?"

Jeremy took a while to answer, as if he wasn't too sure. "Yeah, Mum, I'm okay, I guess. Maybe I should have some ginger ale again . . . *with* the pizza." Careful, he told himself, don't overdo it or you'll be back on a diet of crackers and not much else!

His mother sounded doubtful. "Well, you can try a piece, if you think it's all right. I'll bring up the homework Mrs. Das sent along."

"Did you get a book? About the *Nonsuch* . . . the

ship on the stamp?" But she didn't answer, just hurried out of the room, and he realized he hadn't even asked what kind of pizza she'd brought.

He hoped it was pepperoni, his favourite.

"You could have brought more . . . just in case." Jeremy couldn't believe it. Only one measly slice of pizza! Obviously, he'd overdone the sick boy stuff.

"Getting your appetite back, are you? That's great! You might even be able to go back to school tomorrow!" She sounded much too cheerful. Especially when she started to give him the math homework Mrs. Das had sent.

"Oh," she said, almost as an afterthought, "here's a book I got for you from the school librarian, *Canada Stamp and Storybook*."

Jeremy's heart fell. It was a stamp book. He'd wanted something about the history of the ship. But she had it open and was pointing to a picture of his stamp. Underneath was written:

> In 1668 a tiny 11-metre sailing ship, *Nonsuch*, made a dangerous four-month voyage from England to Hudson Bay to open a sea route to western Canada. Captain Zachariah Gillam with a small crew and French explorer-fur trader, Médard Chouart, Sieur des Groseilliers, arrived late in September at the

southern end of Hudson Bay. It was too late to return to England, so they spent the winter with friendly Cree Indians.

The next spring they returned to England with a rich cargo of furs, trapped by the Indians during the winter.

There was some more stuff about the Hudson's Bay Company but that was all it said about the ship. Not much. It didn't answer everything, but it did tell him who "Médar" was and where the ship was going — even mentioned Captain Gillam. But there was so much more he wanted to know about the ship, its crew and what it was like. Why was this "French fur-trader explorer" working for the English? And who was the "Prince" he and the captain were talking about?

Eventually, he ate only three pieces of pizza. He was just starting on number four when his mother came in and began talking about him going back to school, so he pretended that he maybe shouldn't have eaten so much because he wasn't quite as well as he'd thought. He had to put the piece back with only two bites (big ones) out of it as if he just couldn't manage any more. There were two more pieces on the plate too, looking delicious and just begging to be eaten.

It looked to Jeremy as if he'd have to go back to

school soon, or starve to death. But he couldn't go tomorrow. Mrs. Das had given him so much math it would take him all day to do it.

19.

"Did that book have the information you wanted?" his mother asked when she came to pick up his dishes.

Jeremy watched sadly as she took the two and a half beautiful pieces of pizza. He knew she'd dump them in the garbage the minute she got downstairs. What a waste! "No," he said, "well, it was okay, but it didn't have much about the ship itself . . . you know."

"Oh well, maybe I could pick up another when I go to school tomorrow after work to pick up your other assignments."

Jeremy's heart sank. Sometimes his mother was just *too* helpful.

"I told Mrs. Das you'd probably be away for a couple more days."

He could just see it. Every day, his mother would bring home *more* math and he'd have to stay home longer to do it, and then she'd bring more and he'd have to stay to do that and more and more . . . . Finally, the newspaper story would say:

> EDMONTON BOY FOUND BURIED UNDER PILE OF HOMEWORK.
>
> The body of nine-year-old Jeremy Thorpe has been found suffocated by math. For several months the boy struggled valiantly in an attempt to catch up on his work so that he could return to school but at last he succumbed to the sheer weight of pages. His classmate Charlie Welles was quoted as saying, "We hope that teachers everywhere will get the message so that Jeremy did not have to die in vain." St. Monica's Elementary School is declaring "The Jeremy Thorpe Memorial No-Homework Day" next week in his memory.

He realized he was licked, took a deep breath and said, "Oh, Mum, you don't have to bother. . . . I think . . . I'm pretty sure I'll be able to go back to school tomorrow. Maybe," he added hopefully, "after lunch?" It would take most of his morning to get those pages done.

"That's wonderful," his mother was smiling cheerfully, "I knew you'd hate to miss it. Did I ever tell you how much I hated to miss school when I was a kid? Why, I remember one time . . . "

"Yeah, Mum. You told me." Was she going to get started on *that* again? "You've told me about it quite a few times." He hated to hear about what an abnormal kid his mother had been. "I'll go to the library tomorrow and get the book myself."

"That's wonderful!" said his mother. "That stamp collection has really sparked your interest, hasn't it?" She reached over and picked up the book. "Which stamp is the *Nonsuch* one?" she asked, turning the pages, "Oh yes, here it is." Her face brightened. "I remember this stamp! Your Grandad was with me when I pasted it in." She smiled. "He was so funny about it. Kept saying that it would be an interesting ship to sail on. And something about somebody on our family going on it."

"Did somebody? Some ancestor . . . like on the *Northcote*?"

His mother shook her head. "That's what I thought he meant at first. But then I realized that he meant me! As if I was supposed to sail on it or something."

She was smiling in the sad way she often did when she was remembering. "I decided he was just teasing. . . . He was always trying to get me to use my imagination, but I was a very practical child and wasn't much for games like that."

She gave Jeremy's hand a squeeze. It was the cut one and he almost yelped. There was a sad look on her face. "Then he seemed really disappointed. As if he hadn't been teasing at all . . . and then he said something that didn't make much sense and . . . and . . . " There was a catch in her voice now. " . . . And we never talked about the stamp collection again. I lost interest and put it away."

"What? What did he say?" He didn't want her to feel sad, but he had to know. Why was it he always had to dig for the important information?

"Oh, he gave me a big hug and said something like, 'maybe I didn't *need* the stamps.' Whatever *that* was supposed to mean." She shrugged her shoulders and picked up the magnifying glass.

Jeremy's head was spinning. He wanted time to think about this but right now he could only stare at his mother, fascinated, as she raised the glass to her eye and bent over the page. He held his breath. Would she suddenly find herself on board the *Nonsuch* with that motley gang of sailors? Maybe he should snatch the glass away before it was too late.

At the same time he had to admit that he was just a *tiny* bit curious to see what it would be like if it happened to another person. Would her body just sit there like a lump on his bed while her ghost was back in time?

He needn't have worried. Nothing happened. She set down the glass and began talking normally. "It doesn't look very big, does it? Those olden days sailors and explorers really were something, you know, travelling all that way. . . . " She looked up and began to laugh. "You don't have to stare at me as if I was a ghost! What's the matter?"

"Oh nothing, nothing . . . just . . . yeah, they must have been brave all right. A little ship like that in a big stormy ocean, waves up higher than the masts, sweeping over the decks. . . ." Oh, oh, he'd better watch it. He could recognize the fear and awe in his own voice. He hoped his mother hadn't noticed.

She was looking at him with respect. "I bet you're right, I never thought of that." She looked at the stamp again. "Sixteen sixty-eight wasn't that long after people stopped believing that the earth was flat, and if you sailed far enough you'd just fall off the edge!"

Jeremy looked incredulous. "Fall off the edge? Yeah — sure, Mum!"

"It's true. They really believed that. I guess it's

pretty hard for a space-age kid like you to imagine. But after all, it's been like that all through history. Explorers reaching out . . . across continents . . . across oceans . . . into space. Going out to find places they aren't sure about. . . ."

Jeremy nodded, "Sort of like asking questions and then going out to find out the answer?"

"Sort of. Like finding out there are other solar systems and exploring them. That's just like Columbus, proving the world wasn't flat by sailing past what everybody thought was the edge. That was five hundred years ago, in . . . " She paused and said in a sing-song voice: "Columbus sailed the Ocean Blue, in Fourteen hundred and ninety-two!"

"That's pretty corny, Mum," Jeremy said, laughing.

"That was how we remembered history dates — we had rhymes." She made a face, " . . . except sometimes it backfired because you could get the rhyme wrong and end up with something like: "Columbus sailed the Deep Blue Sea, in Nineteen hundred and forty-three!"

Jeremy didn't say anything. He was trying to think of a rhyme for 1668.

"Anyway, Jer-Bear, I think it's time you called it a day. Do you want anything?"

He pretended to be considering the possibilities,

" . . . umm, I guess you threw away the rest of the pizza. . . . "

She laughed. "I think there might be a piece left. I'll mike it a little."

A piece, he thought sadly. He hoped it would be enough to make his stomach stop growling for food so that he could get to sleep. At least it would help to keep him alive until she left for work in the morning.

20.

It took him most of the morning and three grilled cheese sandwiches to get the math done. It was after eleven o'clock when he finally settled himself with the stamp book and picked up the magnifying glass.

There was a chill breeze on deck and although the sun still shone brightly, it hung fairly low in the sky. Low enough to make Jeremy realize that it was late in the day. Perhaps it was later than it appeared. How far north were they? It could be quite late at night if it was summertime.

There was hardly anyone on deck. Just the man at the tiller on what they called the poopdeck, the highest deck, the part over the captain's cabin. He remembered how surprised he'd been when he first saw the tiller and realized that this ship didn't have a wheel to steer with, the way he'd thought sailing ships did. Just this long pole to guide it. He watched the man steering. It was the man he'd heard the captain call Mr. Tatnam, the mate or something.

The ship had travelled quite a ways since yesterday, Jeremy thought, if the change in temperature was any sign of where they were. The Terra La Bradore the Captain referred to would be Labrador, he guessed. He tried to remember what the map of Canada looked like. He'd have to check it when he got back to school. There was a strait or something going over Quebec into the Hudson's Bay, and that would be where they were headed.

He looked up. Overhead, the main topsail puffed out, catching the wind. He realized that there was another person on deck — well, not exactly *on* deck. High above, on the little platform around the main mast, he could see someone. Was that what they called "the crow's nest," he wondered? If it was, he could understand why. It did sort of look like a nest. A pretty flat one, but then crows didn't make very good nests, just pieces of branches haphazardly stuck together that looked as if they'd blow down in a good storm.

The guy must have a great view from up there. Maybe he'd just go up and see. He knew he could climb up the ropes they called the rigging. And being a ghost had its advantages. He was light and quick, and although his leg was a bit stiff and his cut hand hadn't healed completely, in no time he was there — up in the crow's nest.

When he arrived, he couldn't seem to get his breath. Wow! It was so high up with the ship's deck so far below — and so very *small*! But what a view! Sky stretching out all around him, so high and wide he felt as if he was the centre of the world. And all the rest was ocean. Well, not *all* the rest. In the distance he could see a low dark line far off to the left. That must be the coastline. Ahead of the ship, sort of to the right, were white things. Islands? Ice floes? Blocks of ice? Sort of blocks of ice, he guessed, probably icebergs.

Yes, they'd be icebergs, he was sure. He hadn't realized how pretty they were, a beautiful blue really. And a couple of them were a good size. Hadn't he heard that the part of the iceberg you can see above the surface was only a little part of the whole thing? In fact, he remembered, icebergs were really dangerous to ships. Wasn't it an iceberg that had sunk that big ocean liner, the *Titanic*? You'd think the guy on watch up here would be yelling something.

Jeremy looked, for the first time, at his companion in the "nest." He recognized the Jack-o'-lantern mouth instantly. It was hanging open, showing those unlovely teeth. The reason he wasn't shouting a warning was that he was asleep. And, it seemed to Jeremy, the icebergs were coming closer. Either that or the *Nonsuch* was steering a course straight into them!

Without thinking he reached forward and grabbed Jacko's shoulder, giving him a good shake.

The old sailor woke, wild-eyed with fear at being wakened in such a way. He stared around and then, seeing the icebergs, became even more alarmed.

"Icebergs, off the starboard bow!" he called. "Roust the cap'n! Icebergs! Icebergs!"

"Icebergs! Icebergs! All hands on deck!" called the mate.

Soon there was wild activity below. Jeremy knew the sailors slept in their clothes, but he hadn't expected them to be bobbing up the hatch so quickly. Captain Gillam was on deck immediately too.

"Mr. Shepard, man the tiller!" he yelled, "Tatnam! Shepard! Hard to port!" And the two men pulled on the tiller as another sailor raced up to help them.

"Watch?" roared the Captain looking up.

"Clear on port!" Jacko called beside him. Another sailor was squirreling up the rigging to the crow's nest. It was Perkins.

There was as much activity on deck as Jeremy had seen during the storm, although the ship was not heaving to and fro this time.

Captain Gillam was everywhere, bawling instructions as men trimmed the sails, and once again Jeremy admired the teamwork of this shabby-looking crew as the ship began, slowly at first but then smooth and true, to swing to the left away from the menacing icebergs.

From where he was, staring down into the clear water, he could see how far the part below the surface extended. It looked to him as though it would only have been a matter of minutes before the ship would have struck the hidden edge of the closest iceberg.

21.

The man who had joined them in the crow's nest was Perkins. Jeremy had noticed that Perkins seemed to keep a lookout on Jacko, as if concerned about the older man. Friendly somehow. But he wasn't acting very friendly now as he sized up the situation.

Jeremy had to scramble back onto the rigging. It was too crowded. He didn't want to be bumped off the little platform. He clung to the ropes watching as Perkins grabbed Jacko's shoulder. "Too close! You sleepin' on watch?" he growled. "Cap'n'll have you flogged and worse! Keelhauled! And rightly too. 'Tis death to sleep on watch . . . you'd kill us all!"

Jacko looked terrified. "No, no! No lad, I wouldn't. I . . . I didn't see them icebergs and then . . . " The old man's eyes rolled from side to side. "The ship's haunted, I swar. . . ."

"Haunted?" Perkins looked doubtful but there was an edge of fear in his voice that surprised Jeremy.

"Somethin' *touched* me, Perkins! I tells you it were a ghostly 'and, sure as I'm standing 'ere!" Jacko pointed to Perkins' hand that still gripped his shoulder. "H'it were as real as your own!"

Jeremy almost laughed. So he was a ghostly hand! He expected Perkins to scoff at the old sailor, but instead he jerked his hand away as if Jacko were on fire. The two men stared around them fearfully.

Jeremy was enjoying this. Two grown men afraid of a ghost! And then he heard a ghostly voice.

"Jeremy!" It called from far away.

For a moment he was almost caught up in the same kind of fear that engulfed the two men, and then it called again. It was his mother! So that's what would happen. If somebody spoke to him in the present he could hear them in 1668, faintly, a "ghostly voice." He scrambled down the rigging and ran to the cabin. He had to answer before she investigated.

"Yeah, Mum!" It was a funny feeling being in

such a rush. As if he'd landed in his body with a thump, sort of a crash landing.

"If you're coming to school, you'd better get a move on. I'll drive you . . . ." She came through the door. "You're not even dressed yet!"

"I'll be ready in a minute. Where's my skateboard shirt?"

"Your . . . ? Oh, I washed it — I guess it's still in the dryer." She was going through his dresser drawer now, pulling out a shirt he hated. "Why don't you wear this one?"

But he already had his jeans on and was tearing down the stairs to the basement.

She was standing at the front door waiting when he ran back up.

"What about brushing your teeth and combing your hair?"

"Aw Mum, we'll miss the bell." He had his jacket on now, all ready to go.

Arms folded across her chest, she was giving him her determined look. Jeremy sighed and ran back upstairs. There was no point in arguing with Mrs. Clean.

Charlie was standing in front of the principal's office, waiting for a late slip, when Jeremy got there. Charlie looked disgusted. "If *I* was supposed to be home sick with the 'flu and finally came back to school, I'd at least try to be on time, man! Couldn't you stretch it out until tomorrow morning?"

Jeremy shrugged helplessly. "It was no use. My mother kept coming for homework, 'so I wouldn't get behind' and Das kept sending mega math. So I gave up. And then I forgot my books and we had to go back or Das wouldn't have believed I'd really done the stuff. What's *your* excuse?"

"Went home to get my library book and was captured by a cartoon?" he said grinning.

The two grade sixes ahead of them were arguing that they shouldn't be counted late because they were 'helping put away equipment in the gym.'

"Looks like we'll miss most of the period. . . . What's happening?" Jeremy asked.

"Won't do us any good. Free time for 'research' in Social. We have to pick some historic event and show how it affected the way we live in Canada today." Charlie shook his head. "I was hoping to do the invention of Nintendo but Das said it had to be something that happened *at least* a hundred years ago."

"So you can't do Nintendo. . . . What *are* you going to do?"

"Well, my dad said I should do the battle for the Plains of Abraham and how if Wolfe's guys hadn't been able to sneak up that cliff, we wouldn't have had any problems with Meech Lake because we'd all be French anyway."

Jeremy laughed. Charlie's dad taught at the high school and was always suggesting ideas for class projects, most of which Charlie would rather not do.

"So," Jeremy said, as they finally headed for their classroom, "are you doing that battle thing?"

"Well, I read some stuff my dad gave me and it's kinda interesting, I guess, but I don't think the battle mattered all that much. I mean, afterwards, both sides just sat there all winter and waited for the ships from Europe to arrive. And the first ship that came was English, so they took over, but if a French ship had come in first they'd have been in control, so the battle wouldn't have counted." Charlie opened the classroom door. "See you at recess. Good luck!"

Jeremy wondered what that first ship was called. Too bad he had no stamp for it.

There was no math period that afternoon but Jeremy handed in his homework anyway. Mrs. Das never even looked at it before she handed it back. Great! he thought, I could have saved myself some time.

22.

Since everybody else already had books for their projects, he got to go down to the library alone and look for his. Good, it would give him a chance to check out the *Nonsuch*.

He couldn't believe it. Most of the time he had a terrible time thinking up things to do for projects. He usually waited until the teacher got tired of waiting for him to start and suggested something. He never found the topics interesting. Now here he was with *two* topics he could use. The *Northcote* and the *Nonsuch*.

He was pretty sure that they'd both had influence of some kind.

He remembered the note about the *Nonsuch*.

Hadn't it said something about a "sea route" to western Canada? He remembered Médard talking about getting the furs, and he knew the fur trade had been important.

Unfortunately he didn't know where to start. To tell the truth, he hadn't spent that much time in the library. But he did remember that Mrs. Das had said to start with the encyclopedia. He dug out *The Canadian Encyclopedia* and opened it at the page for the *Nonsuch*. Then with the librarian's help he found more books and began looking in the back reference pages for *Nonsuch*.

He already knew that "Médard Chouart, Sieur des Groseilliers" was all one person. The French/English dictionary helped too. Groseilliers was gooseberry bushes. Now he knew why the captain had called Médard "Mr. Gooseberries."

The "frère" they had been talking about hadn't been Médard's brother but his brother-in-law and partner, Pierre Radisson, who'd set sail at the same time on a different ship, the *Eaglet*. Nobody on board the *Nonsuch* would know what Jeremy knew from his research; the *Eaglet* had been damaged in a storm shortly after the two ships set out and had had to turn back. No wonder Mr. Gooseberries was wondering about his brother. Everyone on board ship would be expecting to see the other ship some time along the way. Things were different nowadays when they could just radio back and forth. Once again, Jeremy was impressed by the bravery of these men long ago.

He was just getting interested when the bell rang. Research, he decided, was kind of like being a detective. He was almost sorry the bell rang. He grinned to himself. Now that was a change. For once in his life he hadn't been waiting for the bell.

"Hey man! What's doing?" Charlie punched his arm hello. "You're grinning like you've been up to something. Want to come over after school?"

Normally Jeremy would have jumped at the chance, but right now he wanted to make another visit to the *Nonsuch*, now that he knew a bit more about what the ship was doing and where it was going.

"Ummm, maybe later." What excuse could he use? He didn't want Charlie to be upset. "I kind of want to be home when Mum gets home. She's worried about Granny, and I . . . "

"Sure, okay. Well, phone me tonight."

Jeremy hurried home. Actually, he hoped that his mother would be late. She had said something about a meeting after work. She had also said something about picking up some fried chicken for supper. Jeremy slapped together a couple of sandwiches to keep himself alive until then and ran up to his room.

He decided it would be nice to try to keep track of the *Nonsuch* voyage on a map. He dug out the atlas his mother kept on the shelf in the living room and propped it open on his desk, leaning it against the wall so he could see it. He wished he had an olden days map. The kind the captain had to use, with the old names on it — like Terra La Bradore. Then he remembered his mother had some wrapping paper with old maps on it, so he borrowed a sheet of it and tacked it to the wall over his desk. He liked the way the old map looked, with the oceans covered with old sailing ships and giant fish and whales.

He wasn't sure what the date of the wrapping paper map was, but it made Canada look like a squished version of the modern one. There was Terra de Labrador sticking out way over top of Terra Neuva. Was that Newfoundland? You really had to hand it to Captain Gillam. He probably didn't have a decent map. No wonder Jacko's job in the crow's nest was so important. He not only had to watch for icebergs but for bits of land that might not even be on the map.

The air was crisper than ever and there was a sharp breeze blowing. The billowing sails hummed above when he arrived on board.

"Time for the men's tot of rum, Mr. Shepard!" Captain Gillam called. "Mr. Tatnam, take the tiller."

Jeremy wasn't sure which man was the mate and which was the first mate, but he realized that these were the officers who helped the captain run the ship. He followed carefully behind Shepard, trying to eavesdrop but afraid to get too close and be bumped. He was getting used to moving about with the motion of the ship but he knew he'd never be able to get around like the crew did and never ever be able to move about in stormy weather.

Still, he was learning a lot. Now he found out what Romieux's position on the ship was, for Medard's friend from Trois Rivières had now joined the mate and they walked to the lower deck.

"You've not had much work as ship's surgeon this trip, have you, M. Romieux? No injuries, no scurvy. Let's hope it stays that way."

They stopped beside two casks, large and small. The men were already lining up on deck like kids looking for a treat. Except it turned out that before they got their rum from Shepard, they had to take a spoonful of whatever was in the surgeon's cask. Judging by the sour faces each man made, it was not a treat.

The sailor in front of Perkins held back and the

older sailor gave him a push. "Take your lemon juice like a man," he said, "and keep your teeth a little longer — you don't want to get scurvy and end up like him." And he pointed to Jacko who stood staring up at the crow's nest, with a strange expression on his battered face.

Jeremy watched as Perkins drank the rum from the dented tin mug Shepard handed him and went over to stand beside Jacko.

"Old Zach went easy on you last time," he said, "but ghostly 'and or no ghostly 'and you've got to take your turn at the watch." He gripped old Jacko's shoulder and growled, "and don't fall asleep!"

"Sleep! I can't sleep at all!" the old sailor growled as he began to scramble nimbly up to the crow's nest.

23.

Jeremy climbed easily up behind him, enjoying the lightness and freedom his invisibility gave him. Once again, he was overwhelmed by the beauty of being up so high. The amazing view, the feeling of lightness, the wonder of it all were almost more than he could bear.

He wasn't sure if it was safe to leave Jacko. Would the old sailor doze off again? There were even more icebergs in view now. He watched for a few minutes. It looked as though what Jacko told Perkins was true. He was glancing around nervously, checking behind him every second or two. Obviously, he would be much too ill-at-ease worrying about "the ghost" to fall asleep during this watch.

Going down the rigging from the crow's nest was

harder than going up. He had to be careful not to look down. Twice he accidentally did and felt dizzy at the sight of the deck so far below. It seemed so small down there as he clung to the swaying ropes. Once again he had an overwhelming sense that the ship with its tall masts, its masses of sails and ropes was top-heavy and could flip over into the water at any time. He hung there afraid to move. How had he managed to climb down before? He remembered what a hurry he'd been in because his mother's "ghostly" voice had been calling. He'd just gone down without thinking. That's what he had to do now. Concentrate on moving hands and feet, looking no further than the next foothold beneath him. He was surprised to find himself back on deck so quickly. That deck felt wonderfully solid under his feet. Amazing that something constantly moving could feel solid.

So far Jeremy had not managed to check the cabin of the *Nonsuch*. He wasn't sure he could do it. Each time he went to the doorway, he ended up back home. Now he watched as Shepard joined the captain and both went into the cabin. He wanted to hear what they were saying but it seemed hopeless. He wished he was a real ghost and could go through walls and decks. But then he wouldn't have been able to steer the *Northcote* or wake Jacko.

He remembered the *Northcote*. He had to stand *still* in the doorway. Perhaps if he moved through quickly he could make it. He did, but in his hurry he almost stumbled and fell down the steps. The officers' quarters were much nicer than the crew's but even the captain's cabin was tiny. He realized he was going to have a problem not being bumped into or stepped on.

Captain Gillam was bent over the chart table pointing to a map as he talked to Shepard. Jeremy decided that his best bet was to squeeze in behind the table. That way he would be out of the way and still be able to see what they were looking at. The map they were looking at was only slightly better than the wrapping paper one. The captain was pointing along a portion marked *D'Etrait de Hudson.* This was the part Jeremy recognized along the northernmost part of Quebec. What was funny about this map was the fact that the Northwest Territories was flattened out over the prairie provinces and there was a sea shown extending down inland. *La Mer Glaciale,* it said.

" . . . wants us to go down . . . " the captain's finger traced a route over the top of Quebec, then south, " . . . Hudson's Bay and winter here." He was pointing to an unnamed river someone had inked in on the southeastern corner. "He's been there overland and knows some of the native people. There's rich fur country, and except for his trip in 1659 no one has traded it. We came this far by ship," he was pointing to the Hudson's Strait above Labrador, "three years ago, but it was too late in the year and the ice forced us to go back to Boston."

"So he's tried before?" Shepard asked. "Why not trade inland through Montreal?"

Before the captain could answer there was a knock and Médard entered. With three men in the cabin, there was barely room to move. Jeremy would have to wait for them to leave before he could get out.

"I can answer that, my friend," laughed Médard. "They confiscate my furs in Montreal. They do not want any trading they do not control. So my brother Radisson and I, we go to the English and now, we have a ship, and," he clapped Gillam on the shoulder, "a good *capitaine*, also!"

"We'll beat the ice this time, at least," laughed the captain as the three men left the cabin.

Jeremy studied the strange map for a few more minutes before moving back to the main cabin doorway and back to his own room.

He spent the next little while comparing maps. The one in the captain's cabin had not had the British Isles on it so he still wasn't sure exactly how the *Nonsuch* had set out. He got a piece of chalk and traced the voyage as best he could. That's what he was doing when he heard his mother downstairs. It didn't take long for the smell of the fried chicken to waft up the stairs and not much longer for Jeremy to run down. He was hungry again.

"So how was school today?"

This ranked high on Jeremy's list of dumb questions people ask kids, but this time he actually had something she might like to hear.

"I'm doing a project for Social," he said helping himself to another piece of chicken. "About that ship. The *Nonsuch*."

As soon as he'd said it, he was sorry.

"Oh Jer-Bear, that's wonderful!" She was *so* excited, she'd probably go on about it for days. "It bothers me that you don't take more of an interest in your school work . . . *and* your assignments. It's because of the stamp, isn't it?"

"Yeah. But I'm having a little trouble getting all the information I want. You know, books at school?"

"You *could* try the public library. There are books there, you know," she teased. "Your grandad always said there were two ways to do research: Look it up in a book . . . "

He couldn't help being interested. "What was the other way?"

She laughed. "Ask somebody smarter than you are . . . and then look it up in a book!"

He wasn't sure he got the joke but just then the phone rang. Charlie to the rescue, wanting him to come over. That gave him an idea and he had the perfect excuse.

"Going over to Charlie's for a couple of hours to work on my project," he said grabbing his backpack.

Charlie's dad was definitely smarter than just about anybody Jeremy knew.

24.

"What do you mean, is my dad in a good mood?" Charlie demanded. "He's in his study correcting papers, as usual. If they're good papers he's in a good mood, and if not . . . " Charlie made a gesture of slitting his throat.

Jeremy looked worried. His own parents had been divorced for a long time and he never saw his father. He'd never quite figured out how a person got along with a dad. "Can you tell?"

Charlie laughed. "Sure. I knock on the door, poke my head in and say, 'Dad?' and if he says, 'What's up?' then he's in a good mood, but if he says, 'What now?' in a go-away-don't-bother-me tone of voice then I do."

"What's up?" said Mr. Welles when Charlie

knocked at the door, and the boys went in.

"Dad," Charlie said immediately, "you know our Social project? Well, Jeremy needs some information."

"Come to the fount of knowledge, have you?" He put his chin on his hands and looked wise. "Smart boy! So what is it you wish to know?"

Jeremy couldn't help but laugh. Even though he wasn't sure how to behave around fathers, Mr. Welles had always been friendly.

"I want to know about a ship called the *Nonsuch*," he said. "Sixteen sixty-eight," he added.

Mr. Welles looked impressed. "Oh yes, des Groseilliers' trip. Not a bad idea for your topic at all. 'The Voyage of the *Nonsuch* and How it Affects Our Lives in Canada Today.' " He leaned back in his chair and nodded. "Very influential, that trip. Effectively opened up western Canada for the English, you might say."

Charlie had been slumped against the door waiting for Jeremy to finish but now he decided to get into the conversation. "des Gros-whatever sounds like a French name to me. What was he doing sailing for the English?"

Jeremy knew that. "He was mad at the people in Montreal because they took his furs away, so he went to the English. Captain Gillam . . . " Jeremy stopped himself. He had almost said, "Captain Gillam said." He'd really better watch it. "His name was Médard Chouart and he was from Trois Rivières."

Mr. Welles was looking at him with interest. "I *am* impressed, young-fellow-my-lad. I'll bet half the history teachers in the country don't know Sieur des Groseilliers' real name."

Jeremy felt good. Charlie's dad didn't suspect anything. He just thought Jeremy was smart. Charlie was looking at him with new respect too.

"So this guy with the big name got a load of furs on the *Nonsuch*, and then what?" Charlie asked.

"Oh," said his dad. "They so impressed King Charles that he granted a charter to the 'Company of Adventurers of England Trading into the Hudson's Bay' —"

Charlie's face broke into a look of amazed recognition. "That's what's written on the Bay store downtown!"

His dad laughed. "That's very good! You just made a connection. You're entitled to say, 'Eureka!'"

"Eureka?" asked Jeremy.

It was Charlie's turn to laugh. "Right! It's when you make a discovery. Dad says it all the time when he manages to find a pair of socks that match!" He turned to leave. "And now we've solved your project:

the *Nonsuch* made it possible for my mother to shop at the Bay! Now let's get to some serious Nintendo before you have to go home."

Jeremy hesitated. "I don't suppose," he asked Mr. Welles, "you know where I could get a map?" Mrs. Das had said that, since he'd missed the first half of the project time, he could give his report orally. It scared him stiff but if he had a map and he could draw a big picture of the *Nonsuch* from the stamp, he thought he could do it.

Mr. Welles was pulling a book down from the shelf.

Jeremy had just thought of another question. "Do you know where the Fair Isles are?"

"Fair Isles? That would be the Orkneys," he pointed on the map. "You can borrow this, but bring it back as soon as you're finished." He gave Jeremy's shoulder a squeeze before he went back to his desk. "You are quite an interesting young man. You've already learned that research is like an iceberg — there's always more below the surface than shows in the final material."

Jeremy remembered the blue ice reaching far under the ocean's surface and all the things he knew about the *Nonsuch* already that would never show in his report. He nodded, smiling back at Mr. Welles. He felt great.

"Thanks. Thanks a lot," he said.

Project *Nonsuch* kept him so busy he didn't have time to take another trip on the stamp, even the *Northcote* stamp Aunt Wendy had mailed back to him. And everything — the stamps, Granny's illness and the trip to Prince Albert — had almost made him forget about his birthday. Almost.

He handed out the invitations early in the week, just in case he made such a mess giving his report that nobody wanted to admit they knew him.

It was terrifying, standing up in front of the class. He was the only one giving an oral report which made it even worse. He cleared his throat. What if his voice was just a squawk?

He turned to the map he'd traced from Charlie's dad's book. Mrs. Das had let him use the overhead projector, so it was blown up big on the screen at the front. Standing there with the pointer in his hand, he felt rather like one of the weather announcers on television. He felt a little better. He'd just pretend that's what he was — one of those documentary announcers.

"As you can see," he began (to his surprise he had a voice and it even sounded like an announcer's), "the maps available in 1668 when the *Nonsuch* sailed from Land's End, England, bound for Hudson Bay, were very different from the ones we have today." He slid the modern map in beneath, so the kids could compare them.

He showed the route the *Nonsuch* had followed and explained why the trip had been taken. He could see Mrs. Das nodding from the back of the room. He was doing all right! He talked about "Médard" and his quarrel with the French authorities in Montreal. Except he said the whole name, "Médard Chouart, Sieur des Groseilliers." He'd practised saying it — he liked the way the French words rolled out.

Then he showed the big brightly coloured copy he'd made of the *Nonsuch* stamp. It felt a little like his "show and tell" days in grade one. He'd actually liked school in those days. He was still talking when the bell rang for recess.

He survived the report even better than he'd expected. He could tell Mrs. Das was impressed, even though he'd wandered off the topic a little, talking about the hardships of sailing in 1668 and about scurvy and lemon juice and icebergs.

He'd survived and that was the main thing.

25.

Jeremy opened his eyes. He always woke up on his birthday wondering why the day felt different until he remembered it was a special day. Today, he knew his mother had planned a terrific party. But the best part of it was that when everybody left, Charlie would stay over . . . for the entire weekend!

So he opened his eyes and waited for the happy feeling to start.

But it didn't. Instead of the pleasant welling up of anticipation for the day there was a strange empty feeling, as if he'd lost something — something important. Quickly he ran through a check list in his head: Nintendo broken? No, he was even pretty sure his mum was giving him that new game he'd been wanting and it was a two-man so he and

Charlie could play it together after everyone left. Good feeling there. So what was it? Bad stuff at school? No, things were going pretty well and, since his *Nonsuch* report, his report card even stood to improve. Trouble with Mum? No, she was holding back on screaming about his room until after his birthday, and with any luck at all there'd be another cool shirt from Aunt Wendy which would relieve some of the "change your shirt" pressure. Besides, if his report card was better maybe she'd stop worrying about him being a drop-out she'd have to support for the rest of her days.

So what was wrong? Why did he have this feeling inside? Like a birthday party balloon that didn't get broken, just ended up forgotten in a corner and when you found it a week later was all shrivelled and puckered and pathetic-looking.

Maybe if he shut his eyes and went back to sleep, he'd wake up properly next time. He was just snuggling down when he heard his mother.

"Happy Birthday to you, Happy Birthday to you! Happy Birthday dear Jeremy!"

He pretended to wake up slowly, but it was hard to do because she was bouncing the bed now as she sang. If he didn't open his eyes soon she'd be tickling him.

"Oh, good morning, Mum!" he said rubbing his eyes. "Is it my birthday?"

And then they both laughed. He always pretended he didn't know it was his birthday, and she always sang and handed him a balloon and then dumped his presents on the bed for him to open.

He wondered how long she would keep this up? After all he *was* getting older. He imagined himself an old man with a white beard waking up on his birthday and in comes this very old lady in a wheel-chair singing "Happy Birthday" in a crackly voice and handing him a balloon. It made him laugh harder.

Then she said, as she always did, "So how does it feel to be ten?"

And, as if he'd been reminded of something, the strange feeling came back. Even as he was reaching for the first present, which should have been the best time of all, there it was — dull, heavy and *empty*.

But his presents were great. Everything he'd expected and more. His game from Mum and two terrific shirts from Aunt Wendy. "Too big, as usual," said his mum. "Perfect!" said Jeremy.

His dad had sent money — he always did — but instead of going out and buying him clothes as she usually did, his mother gave it to him. "I guess you could use this to buy that new skateboard you've been wanting," she said.

So it should have been an all-round perfect birthday. The party was good. Most of the guys he'd invited came, and then he and Charlie played Nintendo until nearly midnight before his mother threw a fit. But, when he went to sleep that night, it was still there, even though he couldn't imagine a single thing wrong in the world.

It was Sunday evening, after Charlie went home and his mother still hadn't said a word about cleaning up his room or changing his shirt, that he began to suspect what was wrong.

"Well, Jer-Bear," she said after supper. "Did you have a good tenth birthday?"

"Great!" he answered. After all, everything had been excellent. Except the feeling and there was no reason for that.

"I'm so glad. I remember my tenth birthday. Your Grandad was so funny. Not funny ha-ha," she explained, "funny peculiar. He insisted on getting those ship stamps of his so I could look at them with him. I'd seen them all anyway and I just wanted to get on with my birthday presents. He kept asking me how I felt. And I said I felt fine. It was a great birthday. Wonderful."

Jeremy waited. Maybe this would help him understand. "Yeah, Mum, so . . . so . . . what did he say then?" He held his breath.

"Nothing really, just seemed resigned or accepting or something and then . . . " She stopped and just closed her eyes.

Jeremy felt like shaking her. She wasn't going to start crying now, was she? "But Mum! What did he say? Exactly." He felt helpless — hopeless.

His mother seemed to shake herself as if waking up. She looked almost surprised to see him there. "Oh? What did he say? Nothing much. At least it didn't make much sense to me." She smiled ruefully. "He said something like, 'Oh well, you don't need it anyway, do you?' I never figured that out." She was talking to herself now. "He brought the stamps out now and then after that but . . . Jer! Where are you . . . ? I just remembered something."

But Jeremy was already up the stairs frantically digging through the pile of scribblers trying to find the magnifying glass, the stamp album. He knew as soon as he picked the glass up that it wouldn't work. It felt different, lighter — like the new magnifying glass of his mum's. But he tried.

He tried the *Nonsuch* first. It *was* a beautiful stamp, the picture capturing all the movement of a ship in full sail. But it was just a picture. Still and dead. Carefully he dug the *Northcote* stamp out of

Aunt Wendy's letter. But he knew even before he lifted it to the glass that the smoke would be still, frozen in time. They were just stamps now. And he was just a ten-year-old boy. The magic was gone.

He felt too empty to cry, which he guessed was a good thing. At least his mother wouldn't come in and want to know what was the matter.

He climbed into bed and lay there, forgetting that he should turn out the light, just staring at the ceiling. And then his mother came in.

"I'm sorry. Talking about your Grandad reminded me. He wrote you a letter before he died. I was supposed to give it to you on your tenth birthday but only if you got interested in the stamps. And I completely forgot." She looked crest-fallen. "I can't imagine how I could have forgotten something so important . . . but I guess . . . worrying about the party and all the excitement. . . . I'm really sorry, I just completely forgot." She handed him an envelope. " 'To my grandson, Jeremy,' it says."

He took it from her, ripped it open and read:

> I hope you have a happy birthday, Grandson. I don't even know if the stamp magic worked for you (it didn't for your mother when she was young), and if it didn't you won't understand this letter. But, if it did, you are probably feeling very sad and confused, and

that's why I'm writing this letter. I felt that way too and I didn't understand, but I think maybe it's just part of growing up. Just one of those steps we take to do it, like learning about Santa Claus! Sometimes the stamps work and sometimes they don't. You can't make them work. The stamp seems to choose you. I'm sure they will help you, just as they helped me. I wish I could have been around to share your discoveries. Mine were wonderful, if sometimes a little frightening.

Jeremy looked at the palm of his hand. The cut was almost healed. He remembered the bullets and the storm.

He folded the letter. The rest was just wishing him a happy birthday and a happy life. Jeremy carefully put it back in the envelope and slid it under his pillow. He'd read it in the morning. Now he wanted to think about it. He shut his eyes.

The stamps *had* helped. The *Northcote* had helped him get to know Granny Stark a little and made his mum feel better about visiting her. The *Nonsuch* had helped him at school.

He wondered what ships Grandad had gone back in time on and how they had helped him. It couldn't have been either the *Nonsuch* or the *Northcote*. Those stamps came after Grandad was grown up. He'd look in the album at some of the old stamps and try to imagine how it was.

He heard his mother come in to switch off the light. "Goodnight Jer-Bear," she said. "Tomorrow, you really *do* have to clean up this room!"

Photo by Mary Sullivan

Cora Taylor grew up on a farm near Duck Lake, Saskatchewan. After moving to Alberta she returned to school in 1968 and studied writing under W.O. Mitchell and Rudy Wiebe, among others.

Cora's articles have been published in such magazines as *Chatelaine* and *Canadian Author & Bookman*. She has had two musical plays produced, and her short stories have been read on CBC Radio. *Ghost Voyages* is based on a short story published in *Canadian Living* in 1990.

Cora's first book, *Julie*, won the Canada Council Children's Literature Prize and the R.Ross Annett Award, and was the CLA Book of the Year For Children in 1985. *The Doll* and *Julie's Secret* have also been highly acclaimed.

Cora has four children, four step-children, and seventeen grandchildren.